THE FUCKING ZOMBIE APOCALYPSE

GRINDHOUSE PRESS

BRYAN SMITH

To Carrie Nicely and Andersen Prunty,
for bringing this one back from the dead.

Christmas Eve on Haunted Hill
Seven Deadly Tales of Terror
The Late Night Horror Show
Go Kill Crazy!
Wicked Kayla
Murder Squad
Last Day
Depraved
Depraved 2
Depraved 3
68 Kill
68 Kill Part 2
Kayla and The Devil (Kayla Monroe: Haunted World Book 1)
Kayla Undead (Kayla Monroe: Haunted World Book 2)
The Killing Kind
The Killing Kind 2
Dead Stripper Storage
Kill For Satan!
Dirty Rotten Hippies and Other Stories
House of Blood
Merciless

PART I
THE FUCKING LOWDOWN

I WAKE UP THAT MORNING and the fucking zombie apocalypse has started. That's not to say I know it's happening right away. I don't, on account of having gotten righteously smashed the night before after breaking up with Crazy Sue.

I know what you're thinking: "Gosh, Phil, Crazy Sue sure is an interesting nickname to give your girlfriend, but surely, it's merely a quirky term of endearment rather than an accurate description of the young lady's personality, because otherwise why would you date a crazy woman for three fucking years?"

Here's the deal on that situation: I didn't give her that name. It was bestowed upon her years ahead of my involvement with her. And, yes, I was aware of it from early on in our relationship. And, listen, I dated her for some pretty simple reasons. She's one of those girls who's so goddamn sexy it almost makes your eyes hurt to look at her too long. She's got a tight little shapely body and the ability to make you weak in the knees with just a glance from those sultry eyes.

Also, she fucks like a demon from hell.

So, there's that.

Sue's given name is Susan Leigh Jones. The reason everyone calls her Crazy Sue is pretty straightforward, really, and it's basically because she's totally fucking crazy. I'm talking a stark raving loon, a chick who should be permanently locked up in a padded cell somewhere and doped to the fucking gills on Thorazine or whatever the fuck it is the head doctors feed the space cases to keep them from going off on kill-crazy crime sprees.

Somehow, though, Crazy Sue had never gone off on a kill-crazy spree and thus was out there walking free amongst an unsuspecting populace. So, you know, maybe you're thinking I'm exaggerating Crazy Sue's craziness. Surely someone so unhinged couldn't have made it to the ripe old age of twenty-two without having violated at least a few of the major statutes in the criminal codebook. Maybe I'm just being a typical misogynistic piece of shit, right? The kind of fucking wanker always going on about his "psycho" ex-girlfriend. Sure, you know the type. And you likely know damn well at least half the fucking time the real problem was the guy in the equation. Guys are assholes. Take it from me. I'm a guy. I fucking know. But, and I swear this on the hallowed grave of my beloved childhood pooch, Dog Juan DeBarko (or DJ for short), Crazy Sue is the genuine article when it comes to brain-scrambled pure-ass-psycho weirdness.

Just because she hadn't killed a bunch of motherfuckers yet didn't mean she didn't want to do just that. She did. I know this because she talked about it all the time. And I do mean *all* the time. We'd be in bed getting it on, I mean really getting into it, when she'd start telling me about her murder fantasies. And I'd be like, "Yeah, baby, that's real interesting how you want to cut some dude's wiener off, fry it up in a pan, and feed it to him with some pickles and horseradish, but bring me them titties."

That worked most of the time. Well, pretty much all the time. It's not like there were occasional exceptions where I'd give in and say, "Okay, let's do this shit and get it over with" just to shut her up. No, I'd distract her some way or other, either by maybe going down on her for an extended period or initiating a discussion about her other favorite pastime, her massive collection of Precious Moments figurines. Seriously, the girl is cuckoo for those fucking figurines. Don't ask me why. She spends an ungodly amount of fucking money on the motherfucking things, buying shit-tons of them off goddamn eBay.

Or, you know, she did until the rise of the zombies.

And until . . . well, that'll have to wait a bit.

Yeah, you'll want to hear all about that. And about the zombies. I get it. Really. Everyone who wasn't caught in the exclusion zones during the outbreak always wants to hear all about the fucking zombies. And of course, you're mainly interested in the other thing.

I'll get to all that. But I need to start with what happened to me at the beginning of that descent into bloody fucking hell. Crazy fucking Sue. Jesus. She's the number one reason I almost didn't make it through outbreak day alive. I mean, yeah, I nearly got devoured by countless flesh-eating ghouls a bunch of times, but that was a direct result of what Crazy Sue set in motion that morning.

Here, I'll share a little anecdote that should illustrate pretty fucking clearly the depths of her insanity. This was about three months before the outbreak. I'm lying awake in bed at Sue's place. My phone starts ringing. I haven't been up long and I'm still kind of groggy. Before I reach for my phone, I pry my crusty eyes open and take a look around. I'm alone in the bed. No sign of Sue. This doesn't surprise me as she's often up and about before I am. The phone stops ringing and my eyes start to flutter shut again.

But the phone immediately starts ringing again.

"Fuck," I say, annoyed by the obnoxious persistence of whoever this pushy motherfucker is. "Can't I get some goddamn sleep, you fucking cocksucker!?"

As I say this, I hope it's not my sweet old grandmother calling because that would make me feel bad and I'm not a bad guy. Not really. Not most of the time. Right now, I'm just cranky because I'd rather get some more shuteye than interact with some idiotic representative of the outside world, even if it's only by phone. Finally, giving up, I reach for the hateful device and grab it off the nightstand. I look at the screen and scowl, seeing who it is.

I hit the accept call button and put the phone to my ear. "The fuck you want, asshole?"

"You should step outside a minute, dude."

It's "Mad" Mark Montgomery, my best friend in the world since middle school. "Why in fuck should I do that, you fucking cocksucker?"

Mark chuckles. "Because Sue is up on the roof."

This makes my eyes open wider. Suddenly I'm more awake. I sit up and start scanning the floor for my clothes. "Are you shitting me?"

Another chuckle. "No, man. The bitch is perched up there like a fucking woodpecker or some shit. It's creepy. I was driving by on my way to work and saw her up there. I thought to myself, 'Hey, man, this seems like something Phil should know about.' So, I called you."

I'm scanning the floor. I don't see my fucking pants. I swing my legs over the side of the bed and start feeling under the edge of the bedframe with my toe. "Are you drunk? Is this some kind of fucking joke?"

"Not a joke. And I'm not drunk. You know I don't start drinking until *after* I get to work. Anyway, you should definitely go check that shit out. I gotta go. By the way, I fucked your mother last night. She wasn't very good. Called your name out while I was putting it to her. Creepy, huh?"

He cackles.

The line goes dead.

I stare at the phone. The guy's probably yanking my chain about the mom thing, but I can't be totally sure. He might be telling the truth. Hey, I know how fucked up that sounds, but my family is weird and fucked up and my friends are scumbags. Harsh, yeah. But true. Except for my grandmother. She's sweet as apple pie. I love that old bag. I hope she'll be all right without me.

Anyway, I drop the phone on the nightstand and drag my pants out from under the bed. I pull them on and find my Mindless Self Indulgence T-shirt. I put that on, too, put on some shoes, and go the fuck outside.

Mark wasn't kidding.

Crazy Sue is up on the roof. She's perched up there in a way I can only describe as owl-like, her platinum blonde hair shifting in the breeze. Sue lives in a relatively small apartment complex. It's not one of those big, sprawling things. But it's situated at the edge of a hip residential area that bumps right up against a busy commercial district.

There are a lot of cars going by and in those cars are assloads of nosy motherfuckers. They're curious about the hot chick perched up on the fucking roof. As I stand there watching her in utter fucking confusion for a few moments, multiple horns are honked. Some dude in an old Camaro leans out his window and shouts something crude.

I show him an upturned middle finger.

Then I raise my voice and go, "Hey, Sue. Um . . . whatcha doin' up there?"

She doesn't look at me. Her pretty face is tilted upward. "Watching the skies."

I nod, as if this explains everything, which, of course, it fucking does not. But she doesn't see the nod so I raise my voice again and go, "Watching the skies for what?"

"Frogs."

"Frogs?"

"That's what I said."

"You expecting frogs to fall from the sky?"

She doesn't reply, just keeps staring skyward.

A silence stretches out, becomes uncomfortable really fucking fast. More car horns slice through the still morning air like a slasher's knife ripping open a prostitute's throat. Or not exactly like that at all. But . . . whatever. Anyway . . .

I try again. "That seems kind of, I don't know, fucking biblical. I thought you were an atheist."

Still staring upward, Sue shakes her head. "I'm a Satanist."

I frown. I've been with Sue a while now. For years. At no point have I seen any evidence of devil worship on her part. Given her bloodthirsty interests, you might think otherwise. But, nope, this is news to me. To my knowledge, there have been no midnight goat sacrifices at Sue's place, but maybe that's about to change. "Huh. That's weird. Since when?"

She glances at me for the first time. She's wearing dark sunglasses. The breeze blows more wild blonde tresses across her gorgeous fucking face. "Since 7:58 this morning."

My frown deepens. "Oh. Um . . ."

"Don't even worry about it," she says, her tone growing stern. "Go back in and make my breakfast."

It's then that I remember the time displayed on my phone's screen when Mad Mark called. "Baby, I can't. I have to be at work in, like, twenty fucking minutes."

She tilts her face skyward again. "Go make my breakfast, Phil." There's a brief pause. "Or else."

"Or else?"

"That's right. Or else."

I scratch my chin and glance off to my left. My shitty old Dodge Neon is parked at the curb. I could get in it and drive away from this insanity once and for all. It's not the first time I've weighed this option. An end to the craziness and a return to relative normality would come as a relief in many ways.

Then I look at her. I study that body. And I think of things she does to me in bed. And I say, "Or else what?"

Still not looking at me, she says, "You can either go make my fucking breakfast and never worry your pretty little head about it, or I can explain at length what's definitely gonna happen to you if you don't do what I want. Now stop distracting me from my sentinel time."

Sentinel time?

Whatever.

I sigh.

I go back inside and prepare a big breakfast for Crazy Sue. I'm almost a half fucking hour late for work by then. Later that day I get shit-canned from that job. No big fucking deal. I hated that job. I'm kind of not the most diligent employee ever, okay? This was at a comics shop. I know fuck-all about comics and superheroes and motherfuckers in fucking spandex, but for some reason they hired me anyway. Probably because I'm such a cool cat and look like a young Brad Pitt at the end of a three-week meth bender if you squint really hard. I kind of made the place seem less like a haven for fucking losers, but even losers can get tired of a cool cat's crusty old slacker shit eventually.

Or so I have been told.

But, I digress.

Anyway, I go back outside to get in my car and drive off to that ill-fated fucking work day and guess what? There are dead motherfucking frogs all over the place. Not huge piles of them, just dozens scattered everywhere. I have to pluck a few from my windshield wipers, which I then turn on to clear away the smears of blood and frog guts.

Weird shit.

So maybe Crazy Sue is a little psychic in addition to psycho.

Anyway, back to where we started.

I broke up with Crazy Sue. Finally. It took months of working up my nerve and consulting with friends. Every last one of those fucking motherfuckers told me in the most emphatic terms that breaking up with her was the smartest fucking thing I could ever possibly do.

Kind of hard to go against prevailing opinion that strong, you know?

Still, none of those bastards had ever gotten their brains fucked out by Crazy Sue. I'm just saying . . . some of them might have had a slightly different perspective on things if they'd ever been dragged into bed by the wildest she-demon fuck machine on the planet.

I had to get drunk to do it. There was no other way. Never mind that I get drunk to do most things. That's a habit. It's my life. But this time it was absolutely fucking *required*.

After it was over—and after I somehow escaped her place with a still-beating heart—I met up with Mad Mark and the usual crew at the Dirty Halo Saloon. In the interest of consoling me in the wake of such a traumatic and momentous turning point in my life, those motherfuckers proceeded to buy me drinks all night long and got me so fucked up I'm pretty sure I eventually became un-tethered from my body and went floating about the cosmos for a while.

And I don't return to my fleshy shell until the moment my mom bangs on my door the next morning and wakes my still half-drunk ass the fuck up.

I pry my eyes open and yell, "What is it, you fucking whore!?"

Mom yells back: "Eat a cock, Phil. That crazy girlfriend of yours just called me and said you better call her back. Or else."

I frown. "Or else?"

"That's what she said."

"What the fuck does that mean?"

Mom snorts. A gurgling sound comes from the other side of the closed door. She's probably swigging from a bottle of Popov vodka. It's her favorite morning libation. The fucking cunt. "How the hell should I know?"

"But I just broke up with her. I don't want to call her."

Another gurgle from the other side of the door. Then a cackle. "You broke up with Crazy Sue?"

My mouth feels really fucking dry. I need to drink about a gallon of fucking water. Also, my bladder is ready to explode. And my head is throbbing. It's one of my worst hangovers in ages, at least since last month.

But in that moment, all I can think is, *Or else?*

I shiver helplessly and a few dribbles of diarrhea leak out of my asshole. I force some saliva into my mouth and sit up with a groan. I cradle my head in my shaky fucking hands. More diarrhea dribbles out of my butthole. Fucking gross. *I'm never drinking again*, I think. Or, immediately revising that bullshit notion for a more realistic scenario: *Not until tomorrow.* Maybe. At the very least, I'm sure I can hold out for a few hours.

Probably.

"Yes," I say, half-moaning. "I broke up with Crazy Sue. Everybody said I was doing the right thing."

Mom cackles again. "That's because they're not the ones with their asses on the line. My advice? Call the bitch now. Oh, and if you go out today, watch out for the zombies."

Before I can say anything to that, the fucking hag goes away, her heavy footsteps clomping down the hallway. I reflect on what she's just told me and almost get misty-eyed for a moment. For a second there, it sounded sort of like she kind of cared a little. Maybe.

Then I thought, *Zombies?*

But I push the thought out of my head. Obviously, Mom's a little more crocked than usual this morning. Such a thing boggles the fucking brain, but how else to explain the z-word nonsense?

I decide to call Crazy Sue. I know what you're thinking. Big mistake to get drawn into a conversation with a girl right after breaking up with her. It's gonna be one endless guilt trip, right? But I figure if Crazy Sue is determined to talk to me, there's no getting around it. She'll damn well talk to me whether I want it or not.

And the longer I make her wait, the more pissed off she's gonna be. Also, the chances of her finally shifting into homicidal mode are likely increasing expo-fucking-nentially with every passing second, so it's best if I rip off the proverbial fucking Band-Aid and get on with it.

So, I grab my phone and make the call.

She answers on the first ring, her tone frosty as she says, "I have George."

My breath catches in my throat at the sound of my hamster's name. I can't believe I'd forgotten about leaving George the Magnificent at Crazy Sue's place. The poor little guy slipped my mind. Between breaking up with the craziest girl on the planet and the subsequent total annihilation of my brain cells via an apocalyptic level of boozing, these sorts of lapses are maybe kind of understandable.

Understandable, but not even a little okay.

I jump out of bed and start pacing about the room, shaking as sweat breaks out on my brow. "Now, listen, Sue. Don't do anything rash."

Ignoring this, she goes on in that same icy tone: "Be here in thirty minutes. Or George gets squashed."

The line goes dead. The silence is fucking ominous. It's like suddenly hearing the buzz of a plane engine after hours of quiet on a bloody fucking battlefield. Only minus any fucking sound at all because this is fucking silence we're talking about here. I feel like some sadistic lunatic has his hands in my belly and is giving my guts a slow, excruciating twist. Diarrhea keeps fizzing out of my fucking butthole. I want to cry. This really isn't one of my prouder moments overall.

I stare at the phone for maybe ten seconds.

Then I grab my wallet and keys and start to run out of there.

Halfway down the hallway, I feel a wetness in my underwear and veer off toward the bathroom where I drop a splattery brown toilet-bomb my twat-gobbling mother can clean up later.

PART II
THE FUCKING ZOMBIE
APOCALYPSE

THE FUCKING ZOMBIE APOCALYPSE IS happening all around me as I rush out the front door of my mom's dilapidated old row house on the south side of town. I remain almost completely oblivious to this for longer than you'd probably fucking figure.

Now, look, it's not because I'm some kind of fucking idiot. A lot of it has to do with being worried sick about George the Magnificent. The thought of my little rodent buddy being squashed beneath one of Crazy Sue's platform stripper shoes has given me a pretty severe case of tunnel vision. Sue does not make empty threats. If I don't get to her place within the mandated time frame, George will be a furry little red smear on her kitchen floor. And knowing her, she'll probably film his flattening and make me watch it at fucking gunpoint because that's the kind of gal she is.

So, getting the fuck across town and saving George is kind of all I can think about. Also, you have to understand the local environment. As I run out of the house, there's a lot of general fucking chaos going on outside. People are shouting. Horns are blaring. I even hear a screech of tires followed by a crunch of impact as a vehicle somewhere out there collides with another one. And then there are the multiple loud pops that can only be fucking gunfire.

Having lived in the bad part of town most of my life, none of what I'm hearing strikes me as unusual. Blood is shed somewhere

15

out in these mean streets on a daily fucking basis.

Mom even warns me about the zombies one more time before I yank open the front door. "They're *eating* people, Phil!"

I don't bother replying. Mom is drunk as a fucking skunk and spouting delusional bullshit. Nothing new there. Turns out the joke is on me, though, because, for once, what sounds like Mom's usual wet-brained crap is nothing less than the stone-cold motherfucking truth.

But, like I said, it takes me a while to figure that out.

A chain-link fence surrounds the little patch of overgrown and trash-strewn lawn out front. Mom's place will never be featured in motherfucking *Home and Garden* magazine, I'll tell you that much right now. My puke-wagon on wheels, aka the shitty old Neon, sits parked at the curb.

At the curb is a bit of an exaggeration, actually. The car's wheels are not exactly aligned flush with the fucking sidewalk. One of them, in fact, is sort of up on the sidewalk itself.

I cringe at the sight of this, cursing myself for the stupidity of driving home completely fucking obliterated. I could've really hurt someone, I guess, or, worse, totaled my fucking ride. But right then I don't care that much. All that matters is the rolling junk-wagon is right there instead of in some bar parking lot. I have transportation, the means to get to where I need to be in order to avert rodent tragedy.

I'm fumbling with my keys as I run, trying to locate the one for the Phil-mobile when I encounter the first of many annoying obstacles. The fence's gate is closed. I hit it at full speed, stagger backward and lose my footing, falling on my fucking ass. Sure, laugh. Be a fucking asshole. I admit, it's not my most graceful moment. It's that tunnel vision fucking with me, making me oblivious even to the closed gate right in front of me.

Anyway, falling on my ass like that hurts like a motherfucker, but it kind of helps too because it sends a jolt of adrenaline racing through me. There's still a significant level of alcohol in my system and it's doing a number on me, but things get a little bit clearer right then. I bounce right back up, grab the keys I dropped, and get moving again.

Out on the sidewalk, a dirty, drunken bum stumbles into me. He stinks like a sewer. Like a terminally backed-up sewer in some rotting post-apocalypse city. Like his guts are decaying inside of him and the stench is wafting out of him in endless, swoon-inducing waves. The wind from the deepest, darkest bowels of hell must stink like this. Included in this toxic stew is a strong reek of piss. It's that cheap hooch all the fucking homeless drink. It oozes out of their fucking pores. Thunderbird sweat. There's also that noxious fucking odor of human flesh that hasn't been washed in fucking months.

I'm talking about a *rank* human being, okay?

This isn't a total surprise. You enter the world outside Mom's house, this sort of thing is gonna happen now and then. Just how it is on the fucking south side.

Yeah, I'm sure I don't sound too compassionate to you right about now. You keep forgetting my goddamn hamster. I don't have time for bullshit like basic human compassion. Fuck that shit. Get out of my way, you stinky asshole, that's what fucking time it is. I've got a life to save.

So, anyway, I give the bum a hard shove and send him reeling away from me. Of course, he collapses in a heap of festering filth and rotting clothes on the sidewalk. I scarcely glance at him as I go around to the driver's side door of my car. I jab the key at the lock and miss. The keys drop from my hands, which are shaking. I'm a little fucking wired by now, you understand. Like I'm on the verge of a total fucking freakout or meltdown and I don't even know about the goddamn zombies yet.

Doesn't bode well, does it?

I scream in frustration.

I kneel and scoop up the keys.

I stand the fuck back up.

And there the goddamn bum is again. I flinch in surprise because he's only a few feet away, right there on the street now rather than flopping around on the sidewalk, which, by all rights, is exactly where the motherfucker should be. The guy should be down for the count but, somehow, isn't.

His eyes have the expected glazed look and his mouth is hanging open, a steady moan issuing from it. I figure he's too fucking drunk to manage anything coherent. He has a thick, unkempt beard. At a distance, he'd be virtually indistinguishable from your average thrift store-shopping hipster douchebag. Lodged within the dense thicket of this bushy monstrosity are bits of partly chewed-up food. The guy probably burped it up while passed out in some fucking alley.

Standard bum shit.

I don't think too much of it even then, except that he's grossing me out. Which, yeah, is kind of rich coming from a guy with wet, diarrhea-stained underwear, but what-the-fuck-ever, man.

The front of his ratty, olive-green army jacket is hanging open. Beneath it is the usual multiple layers of thrift store reject duds. The top layer is a white sweatshirt covered in what I instantly recognize as a whole fuck of a lot of fresh blood. Belatedly, I realize there's more of it in his bird's nest of a beard. Chalking this up to some form of typical bum mishap, I'm not as alarmed by the blood as you might think.

I've got a firm grip on the Neon's key now. I tell the bum, "Get the fuck away from me, you filthy fucking hobo. I've got important hamster business on the other side of town."

The bum moans some more and raises a hand, reaching for me.

I knock it away and say, "Dude, seriously. This is your last warning. Keep fucking with me and I'm gonna fuck you up."

Though I've still kind of got that tunnel-vision thing going on as I deal with the bum, a bit more peripheral awareness of the increasing chaos happening all around me finally begins to fucking penetrate. There's a lot of screaming. The sound of horns blaring is getting louder all the time. There are more gunshots now. A *lot* more.

And then some people go running by on the sidewalk as I stand there. One of them—a pudgy, balding dude—races into my field of vision, stops in his tracks, and spins about nimbly, like the world's fattest ballerina. Or whatever the fuck you call a guy ballet dancer. Fuck it. You know what I mean. He's *graceful*. It's fucking weird.

He raises a gun and fires at something I can't see yet. Okay, this gets my attention. Gunplay going on right next to me? Even I can't ignore this. My head snaps sharply to the left, instinct making me look for his target.

I see her right away. Wearing only lacy black panties and a matching bra, she's a shapely young thing, with dyed-black hair and skin like a ghost, so pale she's almost fucking see-through, you know what I'm saying?

So, anyway, like the bum, she's got smears of blood all over her. A hole in her flat belly gushes more red stuff. The fat man's bullet went in that way. I'm still a bit slow on the motherfucking uptake at that point, but even I can figure that out. So, this hot gothy chick is moaning and moving around all herky-jerky-like, like a goddamn spaz, but she's still on her feet and moving, even with that bullet in her.

I'm impressed. A bullet in the gut? I'd be on the ground, blubbering and crying out for my cunt of a mother. But this gal keeps on trucking, even if she's a bit wobbly. She's fucking tough. It's kind of sexy, in a weird way.

Hey, don't judge me.

The fat man fires his gun a couple more times. Another hole opens up in the gal's flesh, the bullet punching a hole through the space right between her tits. More blood spills in a line down her belly. A chest wound on top of being gut-shot? Chick should be stone dead on the fucking sidewalk, but she's still upright and her arms are outstretched in obvious eagerness to get to the fat man.

The fat man does not dig this one little bit. Looks to me like he thinks it's a load of frustrating fucking bullshit. I kind of can't blame him. The bitch has a bunch of bullets in her and just won't fucking die. The dude squeals in frank terror and squeezes the trigger of his gun several more times, screaming, "Die, bitch, die!"

He doesn't stop until the hammer clicks on an empty chamber. The girl's still coming. She's, like, impervious to death or some shit. It's then that I remember what Mom said about zombies.

I look at the bum.

He's reaching for me. Grime-encrusted fingernails claw at my T-shirt. My freakout-o-meter suddenly pings into the fucking red zone. The bum's mouth is hanging open. The close-up view gives me a glance at what looks suspiciously like bits of partially chewed-up human flesh wedged between rotting teeth.

Uh-oh.

Shit is getting real as a motherfucker. It's all starting to hit home. I'm panicking, man. So, I knock the bum's hand away and punch him hard as I can dead-center in the fucking face. There's a crunch. It's loud. I've broken his fucking nose. There's a big burst of blood. A bunch of it gets on my hand. The hobo totters backward a few steps before falling over on his ass.

Okay, so, like, he's got his hand held out to break his fall, right? Only things don't work out quite the intended way for the undead motherfucker. The impact with the street snaps his forearm. A bone fragment tears through his fucking skin. And then he's got something else in common with the goth chick because the damage to his body doesn't seem to bother him much.

Because he's a zombie, I think. *Holy shit.*

Any other day this fact would immediately seize and occupy

the whole of my attention. But just then an image of my hamster quivering beneath Crazy Sue's platform heel pops into my head again and things are right back in fucking focus. I love that magnificent bastard of a rodent and only I can come to his rescue. Yeah, okay, the world is falling apart around me, but that's not something I can do anything about. But George is another matter. Maybe I can save him.

The bum zombie starts trying to get up again, but the broken arm makes it an awkward process. Twice he tries bracing the hand of his bad arm on the pavement to push himself up. You may not be shocked to hear this only makes things worse for the braindead fuck. The second time he does this there's a louder snap and then half his fucking arm is hanging on by a thread of gristle.

He groans and reaches out for me with the other arm, the still intact one. Recognizing this as potentially very bad news for me, I kick him in the fucking face, snapping his head back so hard it breaks his neck. The sound this makes causes my stomach to knot up a little. I'm still suffering from severe hangover symptoms and this shit is not helping, man, not one fucking bit. But fuck it, I've got shit to do, so I shake the feeling off, get in my car, and drive the fuck away from there.

The road ahead is mostly clear for the next few blocks, except for a stalled Chrysler sedan. This is a big boat-sized ride from the funky 1970s. There's even a pair of fuzzy dice hanging from the crooked rearview mirror. The car's bashed-in front end tells an obvious fucking story, one about a head-on collision, but there's no sign of the other vehicle. Smoke is leaking out from the crumpled hood. There's glass all over the goddamn road. And, oh yeah, there's an old dude's bloody torso sticking out through the windshield.

This sucks for the old dude, but it's not my fucking problem. Besides, I'm pretty sure he's dead already and so there's fuck-all I can do for him. So, I put the pedal to the fucking metal and go around the big Chrysler.

Pretty soon I get to an intersection. This is where things really start to get hairy. A right turn here keeps me moving along on the quickest route to my psycho ex-girlfriend's place. So, barely slowing down, I crank the wheel hard to the fucking right, taking a turn so razor-sharp it barely qualifies as a proper turn at all. The Neon goes up over the curb at the corner, the side of the car scraping against a stop sign.

I'm bouncing up and down in my seat as the tires go up and over the curb and then back down into the street. This is because, not exactly being in a safety-first frame of mind, I haven't strapped on the seatbelt. One time I bounce up so high the top of my head hits the fucking roof. Fucking *ouch*. And then there's a squealing of tires on asphalt as I hit the brakes and skid to a stop.

I sit there and stare a moment.

Motherfucker.

Wexler Avenue is clogged with stalled cars.

But that's not all.

A motherfucking *airplane* has crashed into the street a few blocks up. Not a jumbo jet, mind you. This is something smaller, one of those classic rock band-killing planes. Still, it's plenty big enough to stop all traffic going in this direction and ignite a shit-ton of collateral damage, including multiple multi-car pileups. Of course, a lot of it's the fault of, you fucking guessed it, overreacting motorists.

A lot of dumb motherfuckers are standing in the street and arguing with each other. Maybe they're threatening lawsuits or exchanging insurance information. The fuck if I know. Nor do I give a goddamn because, while they're occupied with this trivial bullshit, other motherfuckers who are clearly reanimated dead are staggering around and taking bites out of other random motherfuckers.

Also, hey, look at this, a fucking *fire* is raging in the distance, somewhere out there beyond the mangled metal carcass of the crashed plane. And this thing is *big*. It's got conflagration written all over it. The goddamn city might burn to the ground. And yet these yahoos just gotta be sure they've got all their legal angles and liabilities and what-the-fuck-ever squared the fuck away.

I want to kill them all. Like, seriously. Because there's no way I'm getting anywhere anytime soon going this way.

"Fuck this," I say, reaching for the gearshift.

I've put the Neon in reverse when something slams into the back of the fucking thing. The impact is hard enough to launch me out of my seat and slam my chest against the steering wheel. The top of my head smacks the windshield. Goddamn. This hurts. A lot. Blood is trickling from a cut on my head as I fall back into the seat. I kind of feel like crying.

But, again, no fucking time for that. George is still out there and needs my help. I've got to get moving again. Before I can do anything about that, someone starts banging on my window. There's some muffled yelling, too. Someone's pretty pissed at me, from the sound of it. Well, I'm not in the best mood either, motherfucker, so stand back and get ready to have your ass kicked up and down the fucking street.

This attitude lasts until I turn my aching head to the left and see a giant looming out there. An *ugly* giant, at that. Tall as a fucking skyscraper, he looks like he's spent the last few years injecting every steroid on the fucking planet. I don't mean every type of steroid available on the market. I fucking mean he took *all* of the shit. All the steroids. There's no more for anybody else. The professional athletes of the world are shit out of luck.

And I still haven't gone into the ugly part. Dude has a bald head the size of a beach ball and a face like a squashed-in pumpkin. He looks sort of like the Incredible Hulk, only with a gross-ass spray tan instead of green skin. Okay, so I sort of lied when I said I didn't know shit about superheroes.

23

As I sit there gawping at him with blood running down my face, he gestures at me, waving his hand around like he wants me to get out of the Phil-mobile so he can better let me know what's on his mind. I'm pretty sure I already know what that is and I've got pretty much zero fucking interest in doing what he wants.

He hits the glass *again*. I can tell it's gonna shatter soon, but I still don't move. I'm thinking I should get the passenger side door open and make a fucking run for it because otherwise this monster masquerading as a man is gonna twist me up like a pretzel. I picture him tearing off my arms and slapping the bejesus out of me with them.

For starters.

I'm about to start scooting across the seat when the situation outside my window suddenly changes. The guy screams, but this time not out of rage. He's in pain. Serious fucking pain. Some kid, some crazed-looking little girl, has popped up out of nowhere and latched onto one of his arms. She sinks her teeth into the meat of the forearm, gives her head a twist, and tears loose a chunk of flesh.

He screams again and staggers away. The girl is still clinging to his arm as blood pours out of the wound. The musclebound freak is waving his arm around and flinging the demonic munchkin about like a fucking ragdoll, but he can't shake her loose. This is fucking amazing. I'm kind of hypnotized by it for a moment. The zombie girl is fucking this big dude up.

I kind of want to laugh.

Serves you right, fucker.

The guy keeps staggering around as the zombie kid tears another chunk out of his arm. This continues until his feet get tangled up in something in the street and he topples over backward, landing hard on his backside. Given the size of the man, I'm shocked this doesn't trigger a fucking earthquake.

I take a quick look around. A white van is behind me. From the looks of it, the van's front end and the Phil-mobile's rear end have had an intimate encounter of the violent kind. They are kind of smashed together. This doesn't look too promising. So when I hit the gas and my car can't pull loose from the van, it isn't too much of a fucking shock.

Meanwhile, the overall situation on Wexler Avenue is deteriorating at an alarming rate. There's a lot less of that oblivious shit going on. Everywhere I look, douche-lords who were arguing with each other minutes ago are now eating each other. I see people running around in all directions, looking like a bunch of dumb chickens with their fucking heads cut off. There are bodies scattered across the street now. Dead fuckers with blood-smeared faces are digging in the guts of some of them.

I've got no real desire to head out into this madness, but I've got no choice. The Neon isn't going anywhere. Also, the goddamn thing isn't exactly an ideal shelter for riding out the zombie apocalypse. The undead are multiplying fast. If I stay in the car, they'll swarm over it and drag me out. I've got to get moving again, but it's gonna have to be on foot.

Goddammit.

So, I open the door and ease myself out. I have to do it gingerly because I'm still in pain from the collision and, guess what, I've gotta piss pretty fucking bad. In fact, my bladder is again almost at that ready-to-fucking-explode stage of things. This kind of crept up on me while the world around me was going to shit.

I feel the urgent need of it with each fucking step I take away from the Neon. I'm whimpering and holding my legs together as I shuffle into the middle of the street. It's not too dignified, but then neither is what I do next.

There's a lot of fucked up shit happening all around me and it's getting worse all the time. People are dying everywhere I look. Screams are filling the fucking air. The streets are running with blood. It's like I've entered some inner circle of hell. But this bladder situation is gonna spell my fucking doom if I don't do something about it soon, preferably right the fuck away. Obviously, I don't have time to look for a motherfucking bathroom, so what I do is, I unzip my pants, take out my wang, and take a leak right there in the middle of the street.

Picture it.

Panicked motherfuckers zipping by me in every direction. Up and down the street. Across the street. Right in front of me. Some are wandering around in a daze, but most are running like the hounds of hell are on their asses. Most of these people are too completely fucking terrified to take note of this insane thing I'm doing.

But there's this one dude. He comes running down the street from the direction of the plane crash. He's weaving in and out around and between the zombies and leaping over the bodies on the ground. This is a kind of young guy in a business suit. He's in this flat-out run, his red tie fluttering in the wind over his shoulder. The speed he's managing is pretty fucking impressive. Probably one of those motherfuckers who runs marathons.

As I continue to drain my bladder, I think about how being fit like that is probably gonna be a huge advantage for this guy in the zombie apocalypse. I'm kind of envious and even a little self-conscious. I try to remember the last time I did exercise of any kind.

It's, uh, been a while.

Anyway, this guy gets closer and is about to go zooming by me, but then his eyes kind of flick my way and he happens to notice what I'm doing. This look of disgust crosses his face, like he can't believe this outrageous thing I'm doing, even with all the other completely fucked up shit going on all around us.

I swear I see real outrage in this motherfucker's eyes. It hits me that he's sort of looking at me the way I looked at the zombie bum outside my fucking mother's house. With contempt. And, hey, I guess I am doing something pretty bum-like, but these aren't exactly ordinary circumstances, you know?

I'm about to yell something defiantly crude at him when the distracted bastard runs headlong into a shambling zombie. The zombie grabs onto him and takes a big bite out of his neck. The fitness-minded indignant citizen screams like a banshee as a fucking geyser of blood jumps out of the big hole where part of his neck was a second ago.

So, one way of looking at it, I sort of murdered a guy with my dick.

But, whatever, he was an asshole, so fuck him.

By then some of the undead types are starting to head my way. In fact, you could kind of say they are motherfucking *converging* on me.

From every direction.

Luckily for me, these aren't those fast zombies like you see in some of the newer movies. They're not banding together and scaling walls in the blink of a fucking eye or anything like that. I think I can probably thread my way through this shambling mob if I just get moving. My bladder isn't thoroughly drained, but I'm feeling a lot better. Good enough.

So, I tuck my dick away and start running. I do a shuck-and-jive thing like an NFL receiver to get by one of the nearer ones and then I'm out in the open again. Relatively speaking, of course. There's still a shit-ton of imminent fucking danger all around, but I'm no longer the focus of semi-organized flesh-eating bastards. That's something, at least.

As I run down the street, I remember the phone in my pocket. I dig it out and pull up Crazy Sue's number, hit the call button. There's no way I'm getting to her place inside the time limit. She lives several miles from where I stand. Under optimal conditions, it'd take me a while to get there on foot. In the midst of all this swirling carnage and chaos, it'll probably take hours. Commandeering another car isn't a viable option, either. I wouldn't be able to steer it through the congestion. Maybe it'll be different once I get on the other side of that crashed plane, but I've got no real confidence on that count.

George is doomed. Not for the first time that morning, I kind of want to cry.

I don't really expect the call to go through, figuring the system is overloaded with all the panicked people trying to call relatives or emergency services. And at first it seems like I'll be right about that. There's nothing but silence coming from the phone for a space of seconds. When it does start to ring, I figure I'll get an "all circuits are busy" taped message.

But I'm wrong.

Sue picks up and goes, "Phil! Where are you? You sound out of breath."

"I'm on Wexler Avenue," I say, dodging a zombie cop as I hop up onto the sidewalk to circumvent one of those multi-car pileups. "And I'm sort of running for my fucking life." I pause a moment to suck in some air. "Look, some crazy shit is happening in the city. You wouldn't believe me if I told you. There's no way I'm getting to your place in time, but I'm on my way, I fucking swear. Please don't hurt George."

"I know all about it. It's all over the news. I won't hurt George, I promise. I just want you to get here, baby. I'm scared."

This almost causes me to take a spill as I veer back into the street, it's so surprising. She sounds not only scared but actually concerned for my safety. In fact, she kind of sounds normal and not crazy at all.

"I'm sorry, baby," she says, voice choked with emotion. "I'm so sorry."

And it's crazy, I know, but in that moment all the unpleasantness and weirdness that passed between us is sort of swept away.

Maybe this crisis is exactly what Sue needed to get grounded again, to come back down to the real world with the rest of us.

"It's okay," I tell her, figuring she's apologizing for threatening my hamster. "I knew you wouldn't really hurt George."

I knew no such thing, but I wasn't about to say that.

"That's not what I'm apologizing for."

I frown. "Uh . . . really? What, then?"

She sighs. "The zombie apocalypse. I knew it was coming. I should've warned you. We could've gone off somewhere to ride it out together."

I almost laugh. "Come on, you couldn't have known about this in advance."

Except then I remember the rain of frogs incident.

Hmm.

"But I did." Her voice is soft, full of what sounds like genuine regret. "I did and I didn't tell you. I'm so fucking sorry."

Again, I almost make the mistake of laughing off this obvious delusion. *Probable* delusion. But I know that'll only piss her off and I don't want to risk losing this rarely encountered semi-rational version of Sue. At least not until I've safely recovered my fucking hamster.

"Okay. So . . . how did you know?"

"Satan told me."

Okay, so maybe semi-rational isn't exactly the right word to describe Sue's current state of mind. Neither of us says anything for several seconds. This is partly because I'm still kind of occupied with the whole dodging zombies and trying not to get bitten thing, but it's also because I don't know what to say to this Satan business.

So, then she says, "You don't believe me."

Statement of fact, not a question.

Yet another multi-car pileup is dead ahead. This time the wreckage is spread from one side of the street to the other and there's no way to go around it. So, I climb up on the trunk of a black Mercedes and start to crawl over it. The trunk lid is warped wreckage and I struggle to keep my balance as I keep the phone to my ear and inch forward. There's a scattering of shattered safety glass on the trunk. My grasping hand closes on some of the fragments a few times, nicking the flesh. Blood dribbles out. I wonder if the fucking zombies can smell it.

There's a heavy-duty Ford pickup truck wedged up against the other side of the Mercedes. Inside the truck bed is a dead guy. Like, totally dead, not zombie dead. It's a tubby dude in a plaid shirt and jeans. He's got a bashed-in skull. I see globs of what I'm pretty sure are brains. My stomach does that knotting up thing again.

"So," I say to Sue as I climb into the truck bed. "You had a talk with Satan and he told you the dead were gonna rise."

"That's right." She still sounds subdued compared to her normal self, but there's an edge in her voice now. It's a tone I've heard many times before. Usually it means shit will be hitting the goddamn fan if I don't watch what I say. "I talk to Satan all the time. We're friends."

There's a baseball bat in the truck bed. An aluminum one. The fat end of it is smeared with blood and brains. That this was the instrument of the plaid shirt-wearing hick motherfucker's demise is obvious even to me. What's not so obvious is why the bat was left behind. Why, in the middle of the goddamn zombie apocalypse, would anyone ditch a perfectly good weapon? Unless, of course, that someone found another, even better weapon. It's the only logical answer. Not that it matters. The bat is mine now, goddammit.

I pick it up by the handle and crouch down in the truck bed a moment, hiding from the zombies and whispering as I try to wrap up this conversation with my crazy ex. I need to be done with it so I can focus on the fight ahead of me.

"Friends, huh? So, what, do you get together for coffee once a week to catch up and chat? Or is this more like a voice you hear in your head?"

There's a *long* pause.

I hear the moans of the dead things as they shuffle about in the street. I also hear the wet, smacking sounds of their feeding. The thing I'm not hearing as much of anymore is the screaming. This is pretty goddamn disturbing. It tells me the zombies are *winning*. Another thing, all those moaning sounds ... they're getting louder.

And closer.

Fuck.

"I'm not stupid," Sue says.

"I know you're not stupid," I tell her. "In fact, you're one of the smartest people I know."

This isn't some fucking lie I'm telling her to keep her calm. It's the truth. Sue is very smart. Thing is, sanity isn't exactly a requirement for intelligence.

"You and your friends call me 'Crazy Sue'. You think I don't know that?"

There's nothing I can say to that. She does know it. And she knows I've called her Crazy Sue now and then myself. Okay, maybe more than just now and then. I don't feel too good about it right then. She sounds hurt. I never expected that.

She sighs. "Whatever. I love you, but I don't care what you think about this. I'm not delusional. Satan is real. He talks to me. And he *did* tell me this would happen."

"Okay."

"Don't patronize me."

"I'm not—"

"Yes, you are," she says, her tone sharper now. "But it doesn't matter. When you get here, I'll prove what I'm saying beyond any fucking doubt. And, Phil?"

I sigh. "Yeah?"

"I'm sorry about threatening George. I was upset."

This brings an unexpected tear to my eye. "It's okay."

"It isn't. I don't want to lose you."

"You won't," I tell her.

The weird thing is, I kind of fucking believe what I'm telling her now. It's crazy. I've spent so many months working up to this breakup thing and here I am, on the verge of patching things up with her.

"Look, crazy lady, I do care about you, you know. You scare the shit out of me sometimes, but you're also kind of awesome. Let me see if I can get to your place alive and then we'll have a long talk about all this shit."

Something thumps against the side of the truck.

There's a loud moan.

Followed by another thump.

"Phil?"

"Yeah?" I say, dropping my voice even lower.

"Was that a zombie?"

"Yeah."

"Are you safe?"

I hesitate a second, then say, "Not really."

"Hurry home. Please."

I nod like an idiot, as if she can fucking see it. Then I say, "I'll try. I will, I mean. I'm gonna hang up now."

"I love you," she says.

I frown, still feeling sort of mixed up about everything, but I sort of have to say it back, don't I?

Fucking right I do.

"I love you, too."

I hang up the phone and tuck it back in my pocket. After I take a big breath to calm my ass down, I stand up in the truck bed. Then I realize two things at the same motherfucking time.

I have to piss again. Badly.

Also, the street is full of goddamn zombies.

In that instant, I'm not totally sure which issue is the more pressing of the two. That sounds sort of insane, I know, but you need to remember that this moment and the end of my night of epic overindulgence are separated by a very short period of time. My last drink before passing out might have been less than a fucking hour ago. So just then it hits me that my bladder might keep on feeling overburdened despite frequent drainings for some time to come. The idea that my need to take a fucking leak every few minutes might be the make or break factor in whether I survive the motherfucking zombie apocalypse is a bit of a bitter fucking pill to swallow, let me tell you.

Okay, you want me to get on with it and stop blithering on about urine issues. I get it. But, hey, maybe you could stop being such an impatient twat? You ever think of that?

Of course not.

Because you're a self-centered cunt-waffle.

No offense.

Point is, this is *my* story and I'll tell it how I need to tell it, so shut the fuck up already and *listen.*

Where was I?

Right.

Okay, so right on the heels of this initial double whammy re-alization is an even bigger mindfuck. You've probably even guessed what it is already. That's right, I'm talking about that conversation I've just had with Crazy fucking Sue.

Like, what the fuck happened there? Did that howling lunatic of a woman zap me with some kind of hypnotizing hoodoo sex ray over the fucking phone or what? Because for those few minutes, all of my completely legitimate issues with the lady seemed so much smaller than usual, maybe even borderline silly and selfish.

But before I can give this any extra thought, I realize one of the zombies is on the verge of making it up into the truck bed with me. Obviously, this solves the immediate issue of taking a piss versus cracking some fucking skulls.

I wind up with the bat and give that first undead taint-licker a smack in the fucking face. You know the sound an aluminum bat makes when the sweet part of it connects with a fastball and drills that fucker deep into centerfield? Yeah, that's what I hear when my first swing lands. There's a crunch of bone as the dead fucker's nose basically explodes. I get some more red stuff on me. By then I'm past being grossed out by it. Getting bloody is the price of staying alive.

The dead fuck topples backward and, swear to Christ this happened, he lands atop the shifting mass of zombies. They've all got their hands up, you know? They're reaching for me because all these undead fucktards can think about is that next gooey bite of tasty human innards. But because their hands are up, they catch this zombie I've knocked down. So now, rather than letting him fall to the street, his zombie pals are passing him backward over their heads.

I'm watching a zombie fucking crowd surf.

Holy shit. Only thing I can figure is it's some kind of sense-memory deal. Scanning the faces out there, I'm seeing a lot of middle-aged-looking ex-humans. They probably attended a lot of concerts in the fucking 90s. This shit is probably second nature to them.

Rock the fuck on.

Anyway, I'm kind of hypnotized by this weird fucking shit for a minute. By the time I snap out of it, a couple more undead cocksuckers are about to climb into the truck. I knock one of them down, back into the crowd of moaning dead things. Like the last one, he gets passed backward.

I can't stop the next one from getting in the truck bed with me, but luckily, he staggers and falls flat on his face. Screaming now as the panic really starts setting in, I swing the bat hard as I can and start bashing in the fucker's head. I hit him several times while in the grip of this fucking frenzy, keeping at it until the motherfucker's head is a pile of unidentifiable pulp.

By the time I stop swinging the bat, there are two more zombies in the truck bed. The only thing keeping me alive at this point is the way they keep falling all over each other. As delirious as I am, I can see that won't keep me safe for long. Pretty fucking soon they're gonna overwhelm me and swarm my ass.

I take a look behind me and see the street now blocked in the other direction, too. I'm fucking flabbergasted. Where did so many of these undead things come from so quickly?

No idea. All I do know is I'm seconds away from being another drooling dead fuck. I've got to figure a way out of this mess, but that's starting to seem impossible.

Meanwhile, here come more undead things falling into the truck bed. Climbing up on the cab of the truck, I do a quick scan of the area. The street is no longer an option. Instead, I'm gonna have to get into the nearest building and make my way over to another street or alley through a back door. There's a good chance the next street will be just as zombie-clogged as this one, but there's nothing else I can do.

Taking the bat with me, I jump down onto the hood of the truck, scramble my way over two more of the many vehicles involved in this pileup, and wind up facing a plate glass window. Through the glass, I see some mannequins in fashionable attire. It's a dress shop. Some ladies are cowering behind a counter. They don't look too inclined to open the door and let me in.

And fuck it, there's no time for that anyway.

I start smashing the bat against the thick glass. The ladies scream. They're looking at me like they think I'm fucking crazy or something. From their perspective, I guess I look it, but that ain't my problem. One of them comes out from behind the counter and starts waving her hands at me. She's screaming something I can't hear from the other side of the glass. Not that I need to hear it to know what she's trying to say.

Tough shit, lady, because here I come.

At least I hope so.

Because this is some tough motherfucking glass. Hitting it produces this weird echoing sound. It's like ringing a gong under-water. The glass kind of shimmies in the fucking frame rather than cracking. It does this, I don't know, the first six or seven motherfucking times I hit it. I'm screaming again because now the zombies are climbing up on the hood of this misshapen pile of metal and plastic that might once have been a Volvo. Their hungry moans are right in my ear.

But I keep swinging the bat, my bladder letting go and filling my pants with piss as my attempt to smash this motherfucking window is increasingly looking like a futile effort. Then, without warning, without even the smallest crack appearing first, the big window explodes inward, raining glass all over the pissed off shopkeeper.

Not wasting an extra millisecond of fucking time, I dive through the space formerly occupied by the window, landing on the floor and rolling to a stop at the shopkeeper's feet. I'm bleeding from several new cuts where the glass fragments have nicked me.

The shopkeeper starts kicking me. Okay, so I've probably got that coming. I've kind of fucked her over here to save my own ass. I know that. But all's fair in love and war and the zombie fucking apocalypse. I'm doing what I have to do to stay alive. To stay alive and save my hamster. And to maybe reunite with my witchy girl-friend. Or not.

"Get out of my shop, you filthy fucking bum!" the shopkeeper lady yells, kicking me again.

She's issuing this directive even as zombies are spilling into the shop. There's a bunch of crashing sounds as undead fuckers stumble through the hole I created and knock over the mannequins I somehow left upright. The bitch is so pissed at me she doesn't realize how completely compromised her former refuge is.

Twisting my head around, I see the dead almost upon us. Several have fallen to the floor, but now they're getting back up and lurching in our direction. The next time the shopkeeper tries to kick me, I grab her ankle and give it a hard yank. She shrieks and falls to the floor even as I'm scrambling to my feet. I reach out a hand to help her back up, but by then the zombies are there and she's basically fucked.

Sorry, lady.

Some of the zombies grab her and start tearing into her. There are ripping sounds as garments and then flesh are torn apart. She keeps screaming and kicking her arms and legs as the blood flies and hands plunge into her guts.

I lurch away from the carnage. Once I get my footing, I start running for the back of the store, knocking over racks of dresses as I go. I hear rapid footsteps behind me. It's the other lady who was cowering behind the counter with the shopkeeper. Maybe she works here or maybe she was a customer. Who the fuck knows? Either way, she's coming with me, apparently.

She points to a door and yells, "There!"

There are two doors at opposite ends of the shop's rear wall, but this lady wants me to go through the one on the left. She sounds pretty fucking adamant, so here's hoping she's an employee and is pointing me in the direction of the better escape route. Here's also hoping she isn't about to lock me in a fucking closet to avenge her fallen boss.

Through that door is a large storeroom. Lots of boxes and shelving. More dresses on racks. And more mannequins. I've always thought mannequins were kind of creepy, but never more so than now. I'm so frantic that at first glance I think these are deader things. I kind of shriek a little, I guess.

But then I realize my mistake. This other lady has her hand on my back and she's urging me onward. I've got nowhere else to go, so what the fuck, let's go this way.

We make our way through the storeroom and reach an exit door. It has one of those bars in the middle. You have to push it to open the door. I'm running full-out when I hit that bar and bounce backward.

I stare at the still-closed door and scowl. "What the fuck?"

The other lady—much calmer now—goes over to a keypad on the wall. She punches in a code and I hear a click.

We glance at each other.

"We don't know what's out there," I say. "Could be another swarm of those fucking things."

She shrugs. "Could be. But there's only one way to find out. And I don't know about you, but I don't feel like hiding out here and delaying the inevitable forever."

Gutsy lady. Kind of sexy, too.

She pushes the door open and steps out into an alley.

PART III
THAT TIME I PUNCHED SATAN IN THE FUCKING FACE

LOOK, WE ALL KNOW HOW this kind of thing plays out in movies and books, the whole scrambling to stay the fuck alive while the zombie threat grows and grows. It's a pretty familiar fucking narrative. And my real-life experience with it went almost exactly the way creators of zombie fiction would have you believe.

Up to a point.

My own story of zombie apocalypse survival wound up in a way fucking different place than anything you've seen on the silver screen or on that fucking AMC show everybody and their fucking mother watches on Sunday nights, including, yeah, your old buddy Phil and his own cunt-bag whore of a mother.

Point is, you've seen it all before a bazillion fucking times, so I ain't gonna give you a blow-by-blow account of every little goddamn thing that happened. Instead I'll kind of cut to the chase here and get to the part you'll have a lot harder time believing.

But first here's the short version of what happened after Colleen and I stepped out into that alley. That's the other dress shop lady's name, by the way.

Anyway.

Back to live action . . .

There are some dead fucks in the alley, but not as many as I feared based on the zombie throngs clogging Wexler Avenue. I see about a dozen of them, but they're spread out. If we move fast enough, we can easily thread our way through them and make it out of the alley.

The closest zombie is less than six feet away as the dress shop's back door swings shut behind us. It turns and lurches toward us. I'd knock it down with the bat, only I've lost the fucking thing in the confusion.

As I scan the trash-strewn alley in hopes of finding another weapon within easy reach, I hear the click of Colleen's heels on the asphalt. The alley only has one open end. I'm alarmed when I see her headed in the opposite fucking direction, but then she drops to her knees next to a green Chevy Malibu parked next to an overflowing Dumpster.

She's got a hand up inside the wheel well and is patting around for something. Being a certified goddamn genius, I guess right away she's looking for one of those spare key magnet boxes. Seconds later, she's on her feet again, magnet box in hand.

She fumbles with it. It falls to the ground. I dash over and scoop it up before she can retrieve it. I open it and take out the key, grinning as I say, "I'll drive."

She kicks me in the shin and snatches the key back. "Like fuck you will."

"Ouch, goddammit," I tell her. "A simple 'no' would have sufficed."

Rolling her eyes at this, she gets the driver's side door open and drops in behind the steering wheel. She jams the key in the ignition slot and fires up the engine. I hobble around to the other side and in I go, narrowly avoiding my nine millionth close encounter with the zombie kind just before I pull the door shut.

She executes a shockingly fast and economical three-point turn and gets the Malibu pointed toward the alley's open end. After revving the engine a moment, she takes her foot off the brake and hits the gas. Tires squeal on pavement as the car jumps forward. She runs right over every zombie in our way, not bothering with anything remotely resembling evasive fucking maneuvers.

It's pretty goddamn badass.

We take a left out of the alley down a side street and pretty soon we come out on Solis Street, another big thoroughfare. There's a lot more zombies here than in the alley, but fortunately it's not yet full of the fucking things the way Wexler was.

Not expecting her to go along with it, I tell Colleen where I need to go. She'll have her own agenda, I figure, her own people she needs to get to, and so on and so fucking forth, so I'm pretty fucking shocked when she says she'll do her best to get me there. After that, I'll be on my own, she tells me, but I'm okay with that. Hell, I fully expect Sue's place to be the end of the road for me in more ways than one, anyway.

So, we drive and fight our way across town, the chaos continuing to spread and engulf the city as we go. There's a lot of swirling black smoke in the air from the multiple fires. I hear sirens everywhere and the sound of chopper blades whirring from somewhere not too far overhead. This is what doomsday sounds like.

Somehow, we *do* make it all the way across town. It requires stopping and turning around and going a whole new motherfucking way several times, but we do finally get to my destination. And the weird thing is how the smoke abruptly clears as we near the area around the apartment complex where Sue lives. In fact, the closer we get to it, the more obvious it is what a blissful little oasis of peace and calm the place is.

Fucked up shit is still going down everywhere else, but it's like there's this cone of protection shielding this one little group of buildings from it. Outside the cone of protection, it's fucking Armageddon. Inside, everything looks normal, except for one thing—the near total absence of any visible human presence.

I say "near" because there's this one guy slouched down in a lawn chair in the parking lot right outside Sue's building. If he's worried about the madness and violence gripping the city, he doesn't show it. In fact, he looks pretty fucking relaxed when I first glimpse him, which happens as Colleen pulls the Malibu to a stop in the street outside the complex.

She looks at me. "This is as far as I can go."

I nod. "No problem. I can walk from here."

She shakes her head. "That's not what I mean. I mean I literally *can't* get any closer to this place. I've been feeling this pressure in my head. It's gotten worse the closer we get. I can't take it anymore. I feel like my head's about to explode."

I don't feel anything like this. "And you're sure it's something to do with . . ."

I trail off and wave my hand at the apartment complex.

She nods. "I'm positive. I can feel it. And something else, like an itch under my skin, getting worse by the second. Now get the fuck out of my car so I can get out of here."

I'm curious about this odd phenomenon, but she's getting pretty agitated and I figure I better do as she says right the fuck now. She's giving off a vibe like any second now she's gonna drive the fuck out of here whether I'm out of the car or not.

I open the door and hop out.

She hits the gas and she's gone without even a goodbye. My feelings are a little hurt, if I'm being totally honest. We shared some moments. Survived the chaos together. And just like that, she's gone in a cloud of fucking dust, like none of it mattered.

Well, fuck it. I'm where I need to be, that's all I really care about.

I walk into the complex and right away I'm struck by how eerily fucking quiet it is. Yeah, I still hear all the shit happening outside the theoretical cone of protection, but it's dimmer now, muffled-sounding. For the first time, I give serious consideration to the idea there really is some kind of invisible force field around this place. Where it might come from and what kind of power might generate that kind of thing, I have no fucking clue, but what other answer to this fucking mystery is there?

The near total silence here would be pretty goddamn spooky even on a normal day. On doomsday it's almost unbearably oppressive. Any other time you'd hear voices, kids yelling on the playground, music, or see the glow of TV screens through windows. But there's nothing at all happening in the complex. All the windows are dark. If not for all the cars parked in front of the buildings, I'd think the place was deserted. Yeah, maybe everybody's hunkered down and locked in tight until order is restored, but it feels like there's more to this than that.

And there's this guy in the lawn chair outside Sue's building. The closer I get to him, the more puzzled I am. I've spent a lot of time here during my years with Sue and I've never seen this motherfucker before, I'm sure of it.

He's sitting slouched down in the lawn chair. A white panama hat with a wide black band rests atop the fucker's head, the brim tilted down over a grizzled face. He's wearing cutoff denim shorts and a red and white Hawaiian shirt open over a deeply tanned potbelly. On the sidewalk next to him are some six-packs of Schlitz in plastic ring holders. He looks to be about four deep into one of the six-packs. The empties are scattered about him on the sidewalk.

He's puffing away on a cigarillo as I step up to him and say, "Hey, cocksucker. Who the fuck are you?"

He pushes up the brim of his hat and looks at me through mirrored shades. Mirrored fucking shades. Like he's a cop in some 70s movie. That fact alone makes me want to punch the fucker in the face.

He smiles and says, "I am Satan."

I laugh.

He laughs, too. "I'm not joking. You want a beer, Phil?"

This weird motherfucker I've never met before knows my name. I mean, yeah, technically it's possible I met the guy while in a blackout or something. I do have those somewhat more frequently than the average Joe. Still, my gut tells me I'm definitely meeting "Satan" or whatever his real fucking name is for the first time. That grizzled face isn't ringing any bells in my booze-drenched subconscious. So, it's kind of disconcerting.

But fuck it, I'm thirsty. I've killed I don't know how many fucking zombies. I deserve a goddamn beer.

Right?

Fucking right I do. And shut your cock-hole if you say otherwise.

I shrug. "Fuck it. Sure, I'll have a beer."

"Help yourself, then."

I grab the plastic holder with the remaining two beers from the guy's first six-pack still attached. The hiss I hear when I pop the tab on the first is music to my ears. I chug it down fast, crush the empty in my hand, and toss it on the sidewalk. I open the second can and take a few big swallows.

Then I belch loud like a frat douche halfway through his first game of fucking beer pong. "Thanks for the beer, motherfucker."

Satan chuckles. "You are very welcome. Have some more if you like."

I'm pretty sure I'll take him up on that offer, but meanwhile I'm curious. "So what's your deal, Mr. So-called Satan? How the fuck do you know my name?"

"We have a mutual friend."

"Yeah? And who would that be?"

But even before he answers, I finally fucking get it.

He smiles. "Why, Sue, of course."

Of course.

My patience with this clown and his shitty Dr. Gonzo impression is wearing pretty thin all of a sudden. I feel a stirring of anger. "Look, dude, you get that she's not quite all there, right?"

He looks confused. "What do you mean?"

I tap the side of my head and go, "As in, she's kind of, well, unbalanced. Up here. She probably needs professional help, if I'm being honest. You know what wouldn't be even a little bit fucking cool, your royal satanic fucking majesty? Taking advantage of someone like that, that's what."

Satan reaches for another of the six-packs and tears a can from the holder. He taps the top of the can with an index finger and says, "Well, see, taking advantage of vulnerable people is sort of an integral part of the whole devil thing. Shit, I do it all the time. But your girl called to me, sought me out." He shrugs as he pops the tab on the can. "And, son, listen, you're underestimating her. Sue's in total control of her faculties. I have *not* taken advantage of her. She's got an unconventional point of view on a lot of things. I find that interesting."

I glare at him, that anger building. "Is that so?"

He gulps down some beer and burps. "Yep," he says, wiping foam from his mouth. "Matter of fact, if anyone's been mistreating the lady, it's you."

"Stand up."

He laughs and gulps more beer. Then his eyes lock on the stained crotch of my pants. "Shit. Did you piss yourself?"

He laughs again.

I'm madder than ever and I've had enough. "Stand the fuck up, you fucking charlatan, so I can knock you the fuck out."

He pushes the brim of his panama hat up higher and gives me this giant grin. It looks a bit broader than it should, his mouth maybe containing slightly more than the usual number of teeth. But I shake this impression off, figuring it's the fresh infusion of booze fucking with my already thoroughly pickled brain.

Not bothering to set his beer down, he gets up from the lawn chair and comes closer. "Go ahead. Take your best shot."

I don't hesitate.

I swing as hard as I fucking can. My fist connects with his

bulbous red nose. I should hear a crunch of bone. There should be a spurt of blood. But there's none of that. And it feels like I haven't hit a man at all.

It feels a bit like I've punched a goddamn concrete wall.

It *hurts.*

And the smiling bastard doesn't even flinch. "Feel better now that you've defended the fair maiden's honor?"

"Fuck you!"

I'm gasping in pain and walking about in a circle, shaking my stinging hand and wishing I could hit the bastard again.

Satan laughs and sits back down in that fucking lawn chair, stretching his legs out as he rests the beer can on that potbelly. "Calm down. It's all good. I know this is all some tough shit to swallow. So, I'm gonna give you a pass on this here display of aggression. Go on up and see your girl. She's waiting for you."

The ache in my hand is pretty fucking severe, but I stop walking around in that circle and glare at him. "You're not the real devil. No fucking way."

Satan sighs. "Whatever, man. I'm done arguing with you. You'll accept the truth soon enough, anyway. Now get your ass up to your girl."

"What are you even doing here?"

He waves a hand in the general direction of downtown. "Keeping that shit at bay until you can sort shit out with Sue. But, hey, man, even I have my limits. I won't be able to maintain this shit forever. So, go talk to her before I actually start to get a little ticked off here."

I sigh.

Whatever.

I move past him and climb the stairs to Sue's apartment. She's waiting for me in the living room. She's on the sofa with her legs tucked beneath her. The only piece of clothing she's got on is my ratty old Sex Pistols T-shirt. Cradled delicately against her bosom is George, my hamster. She looks up at me and smiles as I come into the apartment and close the door behind me.

"Told you I wouldn't really hurt him."

I smile. "I knew you wouldn't."

Then she opens her mouth wide and shoves George inside, making me gasp in shock. "No!"

She grins wickedly at me as she takes my little buddy from her mouth and says, "I'm just fucking with you." Her smile fades as she gives me a closer inspection. "Did you piss yourself?"

"Uh . . ."

She shakes her head. "Go change out of that shit and take a shower."

"But—"

"I'm not going anywhere, baby. And George will be fine." She giggles, her face lighting up in a way I haven't seen in a while. I like it. She's beautiful. "I won't eat him, I promise."

And now that I'm standing here in her nice, clean apartment, away from the noise and terror holding sway out there in the streets, I'm suddenly a lot more conscious of how nasty I feel in my piss-soaked, blood-drenched clothes. Luckily, plenty more of my duds are still stashed away here.

So, I do as she says.

Twenty minutes later, I'm back out in the living room, freshly showered and wearing clean clothes. I curl up with Sue on the sofa and ask her, "So where do we go from here?"

She looks at me and shrugs, that big smile gone now. "That's really up to you. I know what I want to happen."

"And what's that?"

"I want you to stay with me. Forever."

I don't say a fucking thing for a minute or two. The silence is uncomfortable. It feels like it's squeezing me. I look her in the eye and say, "You know what's going on outside. The world's ending. How long is forever gonna be, really?"

She sighs. "The world isn't ending."

I laugh. "No offense, but you haven't been out there. I have. Sure looked like it was ending to me."

Sue shakes her head. "See, but you're basing that on what you've seen in movies. This won't be like that."

"And how do you know that?"

"Satan told me."

I groan. "For fuck's sake."

She narrows her eyes. "You've met him, right?"

"I met a motherfucker in a loud-ass shirt who says his name is Satan."

"That's him."

"Okay."

"It really is."

"Okay."

"Don't patronize me."

"I'm not patronizing you."

"Bullshit. You didn't think there was anything even a little satanic about him? Something not quite . . . natural?"

She's got me there.

I shrug. "Whatever. Let's say that goofy fucktard is the actual, for-real motherfucking devil. That doesn't mean he knows how this shit is gonna play out."

"You're wrong. He does know."

"But how?"

"Insider tip."

"Insider tip?"

"That's what I said."

Another whole minute goes by. I don't say shit, and neither does she. George makes some squeaky noises. He sounds a little pissed at both of us. Can't blame him.

I sigh and say, "And what was the source of this insider tip?"

"An angel."

"Right. Of course. I should've guessed. And what did this angel tell Satan?"

"That the outbreaks will be contained. The zombie uprising won't sweep the globe like in the movies. Humanity will survive. This time, anyway."

"And you believe this."

She nods. "I do. That's why I wish I'd told you sooner. We could've gotten out of the city and gone up to the mountains or somewhere to ride it out together."

I reflect on this another moment. Despite my skepticism, it's kind of hard not to buy into what she's saying. Something not natural is definitely happening here. My still-throbbing hand is proof of this. So is this little area's weird exclusion from the death and destruction engulfing the rest of the city?

"So, why didn't you tell me?"

She frowns. I see pain in the expression. "Because I sensed how fed up you were starting to get with me. I was afraid if I came to you with this, it'd be the last straw. It'd drive you away for good. I didn't want that. But it was already too late, wasn't it? You'd already decided to leave me."

Tears start rolling down her face.

Fuck.

She's sort of melting my fucking heart here a bit. I feel bad. No, I feel like a piece of shit. But then I remind myself of all the rest of it. Those things that freaked me out and made me afraid to be around her sometimes. All that truly crazy talk about wanting to kill people and cut them up into a bunch of tiny pieces.

So, I ask her about that.

And she gives me this blank expression and goes, "What about it? I was just fucking with you. Jesus, you didn't think I really wanted to do any of that, did you? That's insane."

I frown and scratch my head and sort of splutter confusedly for a bit before saying, "But . . . but you're a Satanist."

"So? Doesn't mean I want to kill people. Killing people gets you sent to jail. Fuck that. Fuck that right in the fucking ass. I can't believe you ever took any of that seriously."

I'm starting to feel sort of foolish and more than a little self-conscious here. Sue is talking sense. "To be fair, I do drink an awful lot."

"In other news, water is wet and fire is hot."

"Sort of fucks with my perceptions of stuff, reality and whatnot."

"No shit. So, like I said, where do we go from here? Do you want to stay with me or not?"

I give it a few more minutes thought. There's all the other stuff I could ask her about. The frogs, for instance. But maybe she staged that. To fuck with me. She has a track record of doing that, after all. But then there's all those weird, veiled threats. The vague "or else" being her favorite. I have a feeling, though, that she'll brush all this off in the same dismissive way.

I gingerly take George from her and cradle him in my hands. He chirps excitedly and tries to crawl up my chest. I let him, smiling as I gently scratch the top of his little head. Still smiling, I look at Sue and say, "Yeah, I want to stay with you. I'm sorry for being such a fucking asshole for so long. I'll change now, I swear."

She smiles and kisses me. The kissing continues and steadily gets more and more hot and bothered. No need for a blow-by-blow account. It unfolds the way that kind of thing always does.

Meaning we eventually go back to the bedroom and fuck each other's brains out. Just to be clear.

After it's over, I drift off to sleep in the arms of the girl I'm now reasonably certain is my one and only true fucking love. Probably not the best idea in the middle of a zombie outbreak, but, fucking hell, I've been through a lot and I'm feeling pretty fucking beat. I deserve some kind of goddamn break.

Right?

Later I wake up and realize right away something isn't right. It's still daylight out, but the light coming through the closed window blind is dimmer now. This is how it always looks right around twilight. The sun is going down. It hits me that I've been out for fucking *hours*.

I sit bolt upright and immediately start to freak the fuck out. I'm naked and covered in blood. The bedsheets are soaked with it. A quick examination of my body tells me it's not mine, at least not most of it. I've still got all those nicks and cuts from my struggles earlier in the day, but as far as I can tell, those all stopped bleeding a while ago.

And I realize something else.

Sue isn't in the room with me.

Panicking hardcore now, I get out of bed and stagger out to the living room.

And that's when I see them.

George and Satan.

Satan is perched on a barstool and leaning back against the countertop bar separating the living room from the kitchen. A can of beer is clutched in his right hand. That fucking Hawaiian shirt hangs open over his now blood-smeared belly. His eyes are glowing red. He grins as he sees me stumble into the room.

He raises his beer can in a kind of salute. "Yo, Phil. Glad you could join us again."

Again?

What the fuck does that mean?

I want to scream.

Sue is flat on her back on the living room floor. The coffee table and everything else has been pushed out of the way. Her body is covered in blood. There's blood all over the carpet beneath her.

Positioned above her is George.

My fucking hamster.

Only now he's about the size of a wild boar from the mother-fucking Australian outback. And he's got an erect schlong the approximate fucking size of my forearm. As I watch, he rams it into Sue's torn-open belly.

Satan laughs. "She never saw it coming. Can you believe that? What did she think would happen when she started messing about with dark forces and shit?"

I start to feel woozy.

Satan slides off his stool and comes over to me. He pats me on the shoulder. I notice his hand now has a bit of a cloven hoof aspect. I could swear it wasn't like that before. How he's still holding on to that fucking beer can, I do not know.

And he says, "Go on, bro. Have another go at her."

Another go?

I titter nervously like a fucking madman. Which is kind of apt, really, because it's turning out that's exactly what the fuck I am.

Some of it starts to come back to me. Satan inviting himself in after Sue and I have our reunion fuck. Then the drinking. Satan egging me on in that regard. Sue's increasing exasperation with both of us. Satan's subsequent abrupt cancellation of his budding friendship with my girlfriend. Then that bit of black magic he worked, the infernal mutation that turned George into this . . . this . . . *monstrosity*.

And, yes, I was so fucked up and delirious that I . . . I . . . *participated* in this horrific defilement.

It's all too much.

I pass the fuck out again.

This time when I wake up, Satan and that traitorous fucking hamster are gone. But Sue is still there. She's still dead. Still a bloody fucking mess. I run, of course. What else can I do?

And for a while I'm able to stay on the run. It takes months for the governments of the world to fully contain all the zombie uprisings. And then more time to sort out unrelated crimes that happened to occur at the same time. In a lot of cases, it's hard to tell the difference. Impossible, really.

But not in my case, of fucking course. Eventually, they do figure out that Sue's death was some kind of horrific sex murder and not more zombie outbreak collateral damage. And obviously the law eventually came looking for me.

And obviously they found me.

"Obviously" because here I am, talking to you, getting fed up with your shit again while you scribble your fucking notes on that stupid yellow legal pad. How very twentieth century, by the way. Never trust a fucking Luddite. I'd love to wad that thing up and shove it right up your tight fucking asshole. Yes, yes, make of that comment what you will. It's proof of my unstable mental state, my penchant for violence.

What-the-fuck-ever.

But I swear every word of what I said is true. It happened exactly the way I laid it out for you, every little detail. My dead girlfriend communed with dark forces. She paid a price for it.

Holy fuck, did she ever.

I'm sorry, Sue. So sorry.

And now you're about to lock me away forever because you're convinced I'm nothing more than a raving lunatic. I'm Crazy Phil, right?

Crazy Phil telling his brain-fractured stories again.

But it's true. All true.

I swear it is.

The only thing I can't figure out is how the devil made me do that terrible thing.

PART IV
CLARITY

SOME TIME PASSES. I SPEND most of it doped to the gills on anti-psychotics and, ironically, more out of my fucking mind than I ever really was before everything went to absolute fucking shit. Even in the midst of that druggy haze, I'm dimly aware of a significant amount of time elapsing. Many months. Maybe years.

This bugs me.

Not in a way that makes me overly agitated or keeps me pre-occupied. It's more of a low-key sense of, "Wow. I've kinda been here a while. That sucks." But no one can sense this because for most of that time I show little in the way of discernible outward emotion, nor do I say much to the doctors and staff of the mental hospital, that dreary gray hell of a place where I've been stashed away and mostly forgotten. No one visits me. Not my fucking mother, nor any of my old drinking buddies. Like so many other things during that time, it's hard to know the reasons why. No one will tell me. Maybe they died in the zombie uprising. Maybe they believe the official line about me being some kind of depraved and perverted murdering piece of fucking garbage.

Who the fuck knows?

Who the fuck even cares?

Not me, that's for damn sure. I'm too much of a drooling, zonked-out lump of flesh to give much of a fuck about anything.

I'm kind of like a goddamn zombie, actually, only without the unfortunate craving for warm human flesh. Then something unexpected happens.

The fog clears. I slowly become cognizant of not only my surroundings but also the basic fact of my continued existence on the mortal fucking plane. To clarify, this process takes a while. It ain't as fucking simple as the time it takes to say "the fog clears". The big reason is the drugs have turned me into such a useless lump of nothing. At some point indefinable through the haze, the orderlies stop administering the meds, the effect of which had basically been like having a fucking lobotomy minus the brain-scrambling needle to the frontal lobe. Except not at all like a lobotomy, because this shit is reversible. I'm barely aware of this reversing process happening, except after a bit I do realize I'm not getting jabbed with fucking needles quite so often, and at some gray point that ceases altogether.

Again, I have no idea why this delightful fucking development has come to pass. It takes a while longer yet for the drugs still in my system to lose their efficaciousness. That's a big word I heard on TV once. Have only a dim idea of what the fuck it even means or if it applies to my particular situation, but it sort of sounds like it does, so there you go. You're welcome, compadres. That's what I'm here for, to augment your collective fucking vocabularies. Oh, there's another one. Augment.

Say it with me now, "Aug . . . ment."

It means . . .

Fuck, look it up. I can't do everything. What am I, your fucking nanny?

Anyway, as the drugs do finally begin to lose their grip on me, I become aware of some things, like the fact I'm sitting on the floor with my back against a wall. There's another wall facing me. It seems way too close. Wherever I am, it's fucking tiny. And dank. And dreary. And dark. The dark and dreary part I get, despite the last vestiges of the drug fog still lingering in the blob of long-dormant gray matter inhabiting my beleaguered cranium. There aren't any windows in this narrow space. Kind of hard for light to get in without windows. And if there's an overhead light, someone's turned it off. The only illumination at all is coming from the hallway on the other side of the slightly ajar door to my left.

After becoming aware of that door, I stare at it for a time. There's something significant about the goddamn thing, but at first I can't pinpoint what that might be. And then it comes to me—*Oh, yeah, I'm in a fucking cell somewhere. That sucks. Seems like just yesterday I was a happy-go-lucky guy having a laugh and downing pints at the pub with my friends, and now here I am. How did this happen?*

Other revelations follow closely on the heels of that one. The first is that the cell isn't in some fucking jail. No, that would be far too pedestrian a possibility for the likes of me. I'm somewhere special, a place where they only send the most hopeless head cases. That's right, so-called ladies and reputed gentlemen, I'm in the goddamn looney bin. That's why those guys in the white outfits have spent so much time treating me like a goddamn human pincushion. Only now it's sort of feeling like they haven't come around in a while. Maybe a long while. I'd probably start to fixate on exactly why that might be at this point, except this is when the reason for the "dank" aspect of the cell hits me—it's because I'm sitting in a putrid-smelling stew of my own piss and shit.

Oh, and there's some fucking vomit on the floor. I have no memory of expelling anything from my empty stomach—which is feeling painfully tender, now that I think about it—but the incontrovertible proof I have is right in front of me. A puddle of poorly masticated and partially devoured lumpen bits of white and yellow things that might once have been deemed edible by some sadistic bastard somewhere in this godforsaken facility.

Obviously, I leaned forward at some point and blew chunks. The act of leaning forward probably saved me from choking on my own vomit like some goddamn heavy metal drummer. The hole in my memory suggests this was pure instinct rather than a conscious effort to save myself. It strikes me as highly debatable whether this was even worth doing, but I did it, so here we are.

Anyway, I sit there and contemplate my situation as the last tendrils of that mental fog continue to slip away. I'm thinking clearer than I have in probably a depressingly long time. This again strikes me as not necessarily a positive development. I'm disgusted with myself. Like, all-around disgusted. For having traveled down a path in life that brought me here. One could argue it wasn't entirely my fault, that I was a victim of forces largely beyond my control, but I know I'm not exactly blameless either. I made bad choices. A long string of them. I lived mostly without malice toward my fellow man, but I nonetheless lived destructively. I can cop to that, at least.

This is all bad enough, but mostly this stuff falls into the category of food for later thought. What most sickens me is my current physical state. I don't know how long I've been sitting here marinating in piss and shit, but it's clearly been a while. The more I dwell on it, the more I realize how absolutely awful the stench is. The seat of my pants is absolutely saturated with shit. From the feel of it, it's mostly been a non-stop spew of diarrhea. The front of my pants is one big, crusty, urine-drenched stain.

Stand back, ladies. I know you're all clambering for my ass now. The line starts over there.

But I digress.

This unfortunately very clear awareness of the state of myself triggers a new line of thought. Where is everybody? Why haven't the orderlies been tending to me? I know everyone thinks I'm a murdering scumbag, but a properly functioning mental facility that doesn't want to get shut down wouldn't let this happen.

Right?

Right. Fuckin' A.

It's then that I finally think again of the slightly ajar door to the cell. My head turns slowly in that direction.

"Huh," I say out loud, my creaky voice sounding small and scared in the dank small cell. "That's weird."

I'm a dangerous murderer. A sexual deviant. At least as far as the outside world is concerned. There's no plausible reason why my door would have been left open, at least none I can think of. I'm not even in restraints. I could get up and walk out of that door right now.

My heart starts to speed up.

And that's when someone out in the hallway pushes the door open and enters the cell. I squint against the brighter hallway light framing the figure standing just inside the door until my vision adjusts.

Then I gasp.

"No. It can't be you. You're dead."

But she comes deeper into the room, until I can see her face more clearly. And it's definitely her. I start to feel lightheaded, as if I might pass out. Maybe that would be a good thing. Maybe this has all been a weird lucid dream, an anomalous blip in the midst of the drug haze, a mere illusion of clarity rather than the real thing. Any second now I'll slip back into the hazy mists of dreamland, and this time I'll stay there forever, which will probably be for the best.

This is what I think until Crazy Sue smiles and says, "You're not dreaming. It's me."

Holy fucking shit.

A terrible, cacophonous sound reverberates inside the little cell.

It's me. I'm screaming.

PART V
HOLY FUCKING SHIT

THE SCREAMING STOPS SHORTLY AFTER it begins. Not because I'm done freaking the fuck out, but simply because I don't currently possess the lung power to sustain the eardrum-rattling volume. But I'm still screaming inside, where it really counts. My brain is reeling. I feel overwhelmed. It doesn't help that I've only freshly emerged from a drug-induced state of oblivion so all-encompassing I may as well have been fucking comatose. I'm simply not prepared to deal with a revelation of this magnitude.

I sit there panting and trembling in that self-made cesspool of my own rancid fucking waste until a calming insight occurs. This can't possibly be real. Sue's body was torn apart. She's dead as fucking dead can be, no way around it. Thus, if I'm not dreaming, the woman standing before me can only be a hallucination.

A hallucination doesn't speak well for my overall state of mind, but it makes sense. At this point, I'll take what I can fucking well get. I mean, shit, I've been through kind of a lot. I've been injected with so many drugs even Keith fucking Richards would find it excessive. I've been institutionalized and dehumanized, judged a monster by others who could never handle the truth of what happened for the simple reason that it's too fucking strange and not at all in accordance with what most accept as the natural way of things. I've lost time, what feels like a goodish chunk of my life. Fucking *years*. Who knows what else happened while I was lost in that zonked-out state? For all I know, the orderlies might have been butt-raping me on a daily goddamn basis. Or maybe they were pimping me out like what's-her-face in *Kill Bill*.

I cringe at the thought.

It seems all too fucking plausible.

What all this means, the bottom goddamn line, is that my brain is broken, probably beyond repair. My perceptions cannot be trusted. The things I see—or think I see—are not necessarily real. In that moment, I find this immensely comforting. None of this is real. I don't have to be scared.

I let out a relieved breath. I smile.

Crazy Sue comes a few steps closer. I don't even scream this time.

Why would I?

She's not actually there.

Sue folds her arms beneath her breasts and shakes her head. "Let me guess. You think you're hallucinating."

I laugh. "Yep."

"You're not, though."

"The fuck I'm not. There's no other rational explanation. And you're dressed like a fucking femme fatale from a 1940s noir movie. You never did that in real life."

The bit about her outfit is true. This thing that appears to be Sue but is actually a projection from somewhere inside my hopelessly cracked brain is wearing a tight white sweater with the sleeves pushed up, a pencil skirt, and heels. Her hair is styled in a way that makes her look like Lauren fucking Bacall. There's no trace of all the tattoos she had when she was a real, breathing person. And, oh yeah, she's in black and white, also just like in an old noir movie. So, there's no way in hell this classy-looking dame is anything other than exactly what I think she is.

A hallucination.

"You're not hallucinating," the definite hallucination insists.

"Am so. And that's just more proof. That knowing what I'm thinking thing. Only reason you can do it is because you're emanating from somewhere inside my fucked-up noggin." At this point, I rap the knuckles of my right hand hard against the side of my head. "Ouch. Anyway, I'm gonna close my eyes now and count to ten. When I open them, you're gonna be gone."

Sue sighs and shakes her head again.

I close my eyes. Count to ten.

I open them again.

She's still fucking there.

"Goddammit."

She smirks. "Told you I'm not a hallucination."

"Like hell you're not," I say. "You're just an annoyingly persistent one. Whatever. You'll go away eventually."

Sue comes a couple more steps closer. Right in front of me now. That smirk is still in place. There's something more deeply smug about it now. I feel my first twinge of doubt and with that some of my previous terror comes seeping back in.

"Step off, bitch."

Sue laughs.

And then she kicks me in the shin. The jolt of pain this sends up my leg is real as a motherfucker. In fact, I can't remember the last time I've felt anything so intensely. Probably not since before they slapped me in this cell.

Right about here is where I start whimpering and weeping. Shameful shit, really. But I can't help it. I cringe away from her, press my back more firmly against the wall. It's like I'm cringing away from Godzilla rather than a resurrected dead babe who looks like a throwback silver screen bombshell.

"Stop whimpering. It doesn't suit you."

I whimper.

And I say, "I can't help it."

Then, you guessed it, I fucking whimper again.

69

Sue frowns. "This is not the Phil I knew."

I surprise myself by laughing. "No shit. That guy's as dead as you are. What you're seeing is a shell, a heap of living dead flesh refusing to give up the goddamn ghost for no reason other than dumb instinct."

Now she smirks again. It's getting annoying, that fucking smug look. "It's funny you should use that word."

"What word?"

She smiles. "Ghost. I am one, you see."

"A fucking ghost."

Another nod. "Bingo."

"Bullshit."

"It's the truth."

I roll my eyes. I even start to relax. The absurdity of it all overwhelms the fear, pushes it so far back I temporarily forget I should be afraid at all. It's like I'm back in time, back in the days before corpses started getting up and walking around the first time, and I'm having one of those maddening circular debate-slash-discussions with Crazy Sue, struggling to make any sense whatsoever of the madness spewing out of her mouth like some kind of toxic verbal diarrhea.

"It's bullshit. Granted, that kick felt real. I bet if I reached out and touched you, I'd feel warm, living flesh. But that's the thing. Ghosts don't have substance. They don't have fucking physical form. They're wispy, floating, cloud-like things. They can move through walls and shit. Dissipate like fucking smoke."

Sue snorts. "Right. And what makes you think that?"

"Movies, of course."

"And you believe everything you see in movies?"

I shift around on my butt some, frowning as I become more aware of how truly uncomfortable I am on that cold concrete floor. "Well, no, not everything. That would be . . . ridiculous."

"And you're not a ridiculous person, are you?"

I sneer. "I see where you're going with this. Allow me to inter-ject a perhaps critical admission. At this juncture in time, I figure I'm about the most ridiculous person on the goddamn planet. Doesn't mean I'm wrong about anything."

Sue laughs. "Fine, whatever. I'll break things down to your level. Never an easy prospect, but I'll do my best. Your perception of ghosts, how they behave and what they're capable of, is based entirely on things you've seen in movies. Surely, then, you must be aware of a little paranormal phenomenon called the polter-geist."

"Um . . ."

She laughs again. "That's a spirit capable of manifesting in physical form."

"And you're a poltergeist?"

She nods. "Yep."

"Huh."

Sue squats in front of me. "Listen, I don't have a lot of time. Please focus. I'm a ghost. For real. This isn't a trick or a halluci-nation. I promise. But manifesting at this level requires a lot of energy. I'm only able to be here by tapping into a dangerous vein of supernatural power. And by dangerous, I mean Satan-adjacent. I'll have to go soon, so I'll only say this once. It's happening again. The dead are rising. Some of them are out in that hallway. You have to get up and get the hell out of here."

And as soon as she falls silent, I hear them out there, that dam-nable familiar moaning. And the shuffling. It's getting louder by the second. I gulp as I realize this ghost or whatever is telling me the absolute truth. The fucking zombies are back and if I don't get off my ass and start moving, I'm gonna be chow for the undead. Never mind that I smell like I've been bathing in shit and piss for about a decade and wouldn't make for a very tasty meal. These things aren't that fucking picky. I've seen the proof for myself.

And I'm sure this new wave of living dead has that same singularity of flesh-chomping focus.

Panic surges inside me as I focus on Sue again. "But I don't even know where I am. Not exactly. This goddamned hellhole is designed to keep crazies in, not allow for easy fucking egress. What if I can't get out of here?"

She disappears.

I gasp. A trickle of panic pee drips out of my shriveled dong.

I whimper.

Then she's back again, blinking into existence. But she's not all the way back. She flickers, like an image from an old movie threaded through the reels of a malfunctioning projector. I see strain in her face and for the first time I kind of start to grasp what it's taking for her to be here. She's holding on with everything she's got. It's hurting her. And she's doing it for me. Right about then I feel a super-massive crushing wave of guilt for every unkind thought I've ever had about her. Despite that flickering thing, she no longer looks like a refugee from an old noir movie. This is the old Sue I'm glimpsing here. The one I remember. The real one.

A tight smile forms on her fluttering face. "I've done what I can to help. I opened every door I could before I came to you. It took most of that energy I told you about, but that's almost gone now. I've only got a few seconds. Go, Phil. Get up and fucking go. Please."

Then she's gone again.

This time she doesn't come back.

I turn my head and look at that open door again. It's really kind of a miracle, isn't it? I've been so out of it for so long I can't remember the last time I had unimpeded access to an open door. Wasting this opportunity would be an epic-level fucking disgrace.

I hear another creaky moan.

And then another of those shuffling steps.

It takes every ounce of the meager fucking strength at my disposal, but I manage to raise myself to a standing position. My back's against the wall. I'm panting from the exertion. I feel pathetic. But it's a start. I've got a chance. Probably the slimmest fucking chance imaginable, but it's better than nothing.

I push away from the wall.

Holy fucking shit, I think.

Here we go.

PART VI
TOUGH TIME AT THE
FUNNY FARM

BEFORE I EVEN GET TO the door, I become much more cognizant of how weak I really am. I've gotten skinny as fuck during my time in the funny farm. You've seen pictures of hardcore anorexics, right? They're so fucking thin from starving themselves they look like they could go floating away in the breeze at any moment. It's like that, only worse. I haven't exactly been gorging on gourmet fucking meals for a while, you know. Or vegging out on junk food while stoned out of my mind on good weed.

Anyway, so now I'm hoping like hell whatever I'm about to encounter in this hallway is as wasted-looking as me.

No such luck.

There are multiple undead fucks blocking the hallway in either direction. Five to my right and three to my left. Now, based on that scrap of info, my next move must seem obvious, right? Wrong, bitch. Sure, there are fewer shambling dead creeps to the left, but one of those motherfuckers is the size of a house. And I don't mean like some little house on the goddamn prairie. Nope. This undead cock-face is more like a P. Diddy mega party mansion.

Only super, super gross.

He's naked. On another, more reasonably sized man, his giant fucking dong would look like a third leg. Seriously, that thing looks like it belongs on a horse, not this obese load of festering undead garbage. It sways like a fucking pendulum with every lurching step he takes. Jesus fucking Christ.

Big Boy looks at me with his blank, milky eyes and moans as he takes another step. Now that I'm out here, each of those steps feels like it's shaking the fucking earth. That's an exaggeration.

But only a slight one.

The guy's giant man-boobs jiggle with each fucking step, sort of like the boobs of a Swedish bikini model, only *way* less appealing.

So, obviously, fuck that noise.

I turn the other way.

There's an open door at that end of the hallway. A large potted plant has been placed in front of it to hold it open. Sue's handiwork, I assume. Sounds crazy, but based on what I've experienced so far since coming out of my haze, what choice do I have but to believe it?

The first zombie in this direction is too close for comfort. His outstretched fingers are almost within grabbing distance. I duck and slip around him as he groans and takes another step forward. One of the dead fuck's hands swings slowly toward me, but I elude it easily. In that moment, I may have all the strength of a desiccated dead kitten, but at least one truism from my previous experience with the risen dead remains the same—they're slow as fuck and if you move fast enough, you can get around them easily enough. They're only truly dangerous if you get caught off-guard or find yourself in a situation where they've massed into an impenetrable horde of rotting, writhing flesh. Granted, those things have happened to me before and it could be argued I only survived those experiences out of sheer dumb luck.

But I digress.

Back to live zombie action, already in progress.

The next undead bastard is about a half-dozen feet ahead of

me. He's a bit more substantial than the rather more waifish zombie I just eluded, but he's not quite the lurching behemoth blocking the other direction. He's about six feet tall and wearing the white scrubs of an orderly. There are several rents in the fabric of the white tunic, which is stained a deep crimson with a large amount of dried blood. One of his eyes are gone. There are more holes in his throat and in his cheeks. Somebody—some real pissed-off motherfucker, from the looks of it—took a knife to this dude and went to fucking town.

He reaches for me. His fingers snag the fabric of my jumpsuit as I attempt to duck and move past him. For a second, I panic. I'm thinking I'm about to be zombie chow for sure. The dead fuck pulls me closer. My terror gets the adrenaline flowing and I find I've got more strength remaining than I thought. Not much, mind you, but enough to lurch backward and avoid the zombie's gnashing teeth as he tries to take a bite out of my throat. The shoulder of my jumpsuit tears and the sleeve comes off as I stumble away. Last I see of it, the zombie is staring in a confused way at the wad of fabric clutched tight in its hand.

Next up in the undead parade is a much smaller specimen. A girl. She's tiny, thin as fuck—thinner than me, even, the poor fucking thing—and maybe a hair over five feet. She has stringy, lank blonde hair and the usual dead, empty look in her eyes. She's wearing a thin hospital gown. The poor thing looks like she's drowning in the garment. I'm guessing she's a patient, like me, though probably from another wing of the facility, judging from that gown. She's pitiful.

I almost feel sorry for her.

Until she lets out a growl and lunges at me. It's like my dear old grandmother used to say, appearances can be deceiving, especially when you're dealing with dirty, underhanded bitches. My grandma was a bit of a self-loathing misogynist. According to her, that description applied to most women. Anyway, this undead dirty bitch looks frailer than the rest of these things put together, but turns out she's the liveliest of them by far. I shriek and back-pedal away from her, stumbling and falling against the wall to my left. But she's still coming at me. She's got her hands on my left wrist. Her mouth is open and about to snap shut on warm flesh. In the last second before she can doom me to a bleak future as a drooling, flesh-eating ghoul, I knee her in the stomach and send her flying backward. More of that new, adrenaline-fueled strength at work.

But she comes right back at me.

"Goddammit," I say, getting annoyed.

I sidestep as she gets close and grab a fistful of the hair at the back of her head. Her momentum helps as I smash her face into the wall. She's still flailing. The one blow's not gonna be enough. I pull her head back. There's a wet red smear on the wall. It's a bigger and darker smear after I bash her head against the wall a few more times. Honestly, I kind of lose count how many times I bounce her formerly pretty face off that hard surface. This is more frustration boiling out and seeking release through the most im-mediate means available, which happens to be pulverizing this dead chick's face. I feel kind of bad about it for a fraction of a sec-ond after I finally let go of her and her limp body drops to the floor.

The feeling passes in record fucking time, though, because an-other living dead bitch is almost right up on my ass. This one's a middle-aged woman. Or was a middle-aged woman. Whatever. She's plumper than the girl whose face I've just turned into fuck-ing mush. I wheel about and bump her away with the thrust of a bony forearm. She falls over on her ass. I hear brittle bones break. Good. Hip bones, her pelvis, something like that. Bottom line, she's not getting back. There's one more zombie standing be-tween me and that open door. I freeze for a second when it hits me who it is—Dr. Ramsey, the head-shrinker who was primarily responsible for my care when I first came to this place.

The scum-sucking bastard.

He's attired in his usual pretentious douche-lord outfit—a beige suede jacket with patches on the elbows over a blue button-down shirt, a thin red tie, and faded blue jeans to make him look more like a man of the people rather than the overly educated, snooty cocksucker he actually is. Topping it off, a pair of wire-rim glasses designed to kind of remind you of John fucking Lennon. You've seen guys like Dr. Ramsey before, I'm sure. The universities of this nation are overrun with this particular strain of self-consciously quirky vermin. It's a look that's supposed to say, "Hey, look at me, I'm a fucking egghead, but I'm also down-to-earth and relatable. All cute and bangable co-ed babes may now commence forming an orderly line outside my office door."

A-hem.

I digress. Again. It's possible I have some unresolved issues related to my own brief and inglorious experiences within the halls of higher learning.

Anyway, once the shock of the moment passes, I can't help laughing. "Ramsey, you living dead fuck. I'm gonna enjoy this."

I wind up and kick him in the balls. Then I frown, because this has no effect whatsoever. Well, that's not precisely true. He does stagger back a couple steps. But he doesn't fall over and he doesn't howl in pain. Of course he doesn't, because I immediately realize I've made the mistake of still thinking of Ramsey as human. But he's not human at all anymore, even if he looks it. He's a fucking zombie and, not being fucking alive anymore, doesn't feel pain.

Ramsey comes lurching at me again, but I've learned my lesson and this time I duck under his outstretched arms and make a dash for that door. I turn around as I get there and survey the hallway behind me. The remaining zombies are closer than I expect. I grimace. A shiver goes through me. Yeah, they're slow as fuck, but they're not exactly standing still either. If you fuck around like I just did with Ramsey, they can catch up with you faster than you'd imagine.

I kick that potted plant out of the way, slip through the doorway, and throw the heavy steel door shut. I'm in a stairwell. It's empty as far as I can see, which is obviously fucking awesome. No zombies in the way means no immediate danger and that's nice after my close calls in the hallway. That's the good news. The bad news is I kicked that big plant out of the way with a bare foot. I look down. Sure enough, I am unshod. That means I've got no shoes on my goddamn feet. My toenails are long, downward-curved, and quite gnarly-looking. They are the feet of a fucking caveman. Gross.

Super, super gross.

I stand there grimacing in pain with my back against the door for several moments as I wait for the worst of the pain to recede. When it does, I hobble over to the edge of the next set of stairs going down. Again, nothing down there I can see. Maybe the universe is finally cutting me some slack for a change. Before I start down the stairs, I take a look around to make sure I'm not missing any angles here. There's another set of stairs going up. I want out of this fucking place and see no benefit in going that way. But there's a big window behind me, presumably with a view of the grounds of the facility. Figuring it'd be a good idea to get a lay of the land before I do anything else, I hobble over to the window and take a peek outside.

Gulp.

My view is of the rear grounds. Straight down, there's a Dumpster adjacent to a door I figure is normally accessible only to employees. There's also a parking lot and a couple dozen vehicles. Parking for employees, I reckon. Beyond the parking lot is a large green field. A tall chain-link fence separates the lot from the field. There are benches out there and some tables. Looks like a place where the hospital's more manageable patients might be taken for daily exercise. And a bunch of those patients are out there right now. More are down there in the parking lot, along with several people wearing staff uniforms. And, you guessed it, they are all walking dead fuckers.

Goddammit.

This is obviously upsetting as hell, but there's a bit of an upside. Yeah, there's a lot of them, but not enough to form those impenetrable walls of flesh I ran into in the city that first time around. There's space to run and maybe zig-zag my way through them.

If I'm fast enough.

Which brings us back around to the problem of my bare feet. Doesn't take me long to conclude I won't get far like this. All it'd take is one step on a stray nail to bring me down. And after that the zombies would be on me fast. Yeah, there's some room to maneuver if I'm moving fast enough, but not much. Even one tumble would uncomfortably reduce my margin of error.

So, I decide to head up to the next floor instead. I grab on to the stair rail and wince as I heave myself up the stairs. In a few moments, I've made it to the next floor landing. Another door propped open by a large potted plant. Sue's doing again, I suppose. Where she's getting all these giant potted plants from, I have no idea, but whatever. Anyway, there's probably gonna be more dead things through that door.

But fuck it.

There's gonna be zombies practically everywhere I turn. I can't let that sway me.

I heave another breath and go on through the door. To my deep astonishment, this one's free of reanimated dead. There are no living humans in sight, either. The rooms ahead look empty as fuck. There's what looks like an employee break room to my left and a small lounge area with a TV mounted on the wall to my right. The TV is on, but it's showing only static. Hard not to take that any way other than ominous as all fuck.

The hallway beyond this area does not appear to be lined with cells. There are doors, but they're not forbidding slabs of reinforced steel. Noting a red phone on a wall in the break room, I head that way and lift the receiver off the hook.

No dial tone. Of fucking course.

I let the receiver slip from my fingers rather than putting it back on the hook, because what's the point? Sue told me it was happening again, but she neglected to fill me in on how far gone things had already gotten. The power's still on, somehow, but everything else is falling apart. No phone service. Nothing on the TV. And from the looks of things outside, about everybody else is dead now. I tell myself this is one tiny corner of the world and things might be different elsewhere, but I derive little comfort at all from this because my gut is telling me something else altogether.

The first time was a dry run. We were all deluded into thinking the powers-that-be had a handle on it and the threat was over for good. No dice. This right here, ladies and gents, is the real fucking zombie apocalypse. And it's looking like there's not gonna be any way out. Not for me or anyone else in this rotten fucking world. Still, I've got to try. As long as there's breath in me, I will keep moving forward. Because even after all I've been through, I'm still human. And mostly we keep going, even after all looks lost.

I pass through the break area into the hallway beyond. Right away, I see that a lot of the doors ahead of me are standing open. I pause at the first one and look inside. It looks like an exam room. In the middle of it is one of those cushioned exam tables with a roll of sanitary paper at the end. At some point in the recent past, a length of the paper had been stretched out over the table's cushioned surface. At some point after that, the length of paper somehow got shredded and spattered with blood. My best guess is this likely had something to do with the two dead motherfuckers on the floor.

These guys aren't zombies. They are for-real dead. Thank fuck. I'm still exhausted from the series of close calls that ensued after fleeing my room. Last thing I need right now is to tangle with dead fuckers again. Some kind of desperate struggle went down in here. Various medical exam tools are scattered all over the room. One of them is a scalpel coated in dried blood. It's on the floor near the outstretched fingers of one of the dead men, a guy wearing the jumpsuit of a patient. The garment looks kind of like the one I'm wearing, only it isn't coated in a disgusting combination of diarrhea, piss, and fucking puke. There's some blood spattered across the front of it, but otherwise it looks pristine. And the guy looks about my size. I consider switching out my jumpsuit for the dead guy's somewhat less sickening one, only it occurs to me maybe I don't want to be immediately identifiable as an escaped mental patient should I somehow manage to get out of this fucking place.

That brings us to the other dead guy. He's also more or less in the same size range as yours fucking truly, only his build is a bit beefier. Not fat, exactly, but definitely bigger than me, especially now I've involuntarily spent so long on the drooling vegetable diet. I won't quite drown in this dude's duds, but they'll hang off me in a sloppy-looking way. However, looking well put-together isn't a top priority, as you might have guessed. This guy is wearing a white lab coat over his regular clothes. It's also got a generous spattering of blood across the front. Another fucking doctor. Beneath the lab coat, he's wearing blue jeans, a white button-up shirt, and a tie. Thankfully, there's a belt around his waist. At least I won't have to awkwardly walk around holding the jeans up by the belt loops, which is the kind of thing that could impede the effective eluding of zombies to a perhaps fatal degree.

The dead doctor is sitting slumped against the far wall near a window. Splattered messily on the wall behind him is a combination of dried blood, bone fragments, and globs of stuff I guess are bits of the dead man's brains. Clutched in his right hand is a handgun. It's easy to guess the basics of what happened here. One of the doctor's patients, this other dead guy, went zombie on him. The zombie nicked him several times with the scalpel. Or . . . wait, zombies aren't really known for their fine motor skills. Using tools or things like scalpels as weapons is pretty much beyond them. So maybe this guy was still human during this altercation. Weird. I spend a few moments pondering why two living human beings would be trying to kill each other in the middle of a zombie uprising. One would think they'd put their differences aside and band together to fight the dead fuckers. Then I remember I'm in the fucking looney bin. The deeply damaged people warehoused here aren't known for their rationality. The fight might have been over nothing at all, at least at the start. Crazy guy just snaps and tries to do crazy stuff. But the doctor's got a piece on him. Bang, bang. It's all fucking over. But the doctor knows the world around him is fucked. He doesn't think he can face it. Or maybe he even feels remorse over killing one of his patients. Probably not, but you never fucking know.

So, he puts the gun in his mouth and BOOM.

Bye, bye doctor.

I kneel and grab the dead doc by his ankles, grunting and grimacing as I pull him away from the blood-spattered wall. Some of his gore-soaked hair sticks to the wall a moment before coming free with an audible ripping sound. The gun tumbles from the man's limp, dead fingers and hits the white-tiled floor with a loud clatter. I cringe for a second, fearing it might go off and send a bullet ricocheting around the room. Doesn't happen, fortunately, and I drag the doc closer to the center of the room.

Pulling the man away from the wall is the hardest I've exerted myself in forever. The doc probably weighed somewhere around one-hundred and eighty pounds, give or take, a rough guess based on what I used to weigh back in the good old bad days, which was a bit less than that. It's a lot of dead weight for such a scrawny piece of nothing in rough shape to be hauling around. Before I can begin the grim fucking task of undressing the corpse, I need a few moments to catch my breath and wipe the sweat from my brow. As I lean against the exam table, I can feel the jackhammering of my heart. Seems to take forever to slow back to a normal rate.

Finally does, though, and I waste no additional time getting down to the nasty fucking business at hand. It's gonna wear me out again, even more this time, but it's got to be done. This is the perfect opportunity to at least somewhat improve the state of my person and maybe start feeling like a real fucking human being again. I'm not about to pass it up. That the chance has even presented itself feels a touch miraculous. But I know that's bullshit. This isn't divine intervention. If God exists, I've got to be the last person on the planet He's interested in helping. I'm a scumbag piece of shit. I mean, come the fuck on. Even I know that. This is nothing but a fluke, a rare turn of good luck.

I kneel next to the dead man and work at getting the lab coat off him first. This involves a lot of heaving, turning, and twisting of the corpse. It's gross. The corpse makes some gross noises to emphasize the grossness, including a belch from beyond the grave so miserably awful the stench of it briefly overwhelms my own stink. The tie knotted around the man's neck makes for an effective leveraging tool. I'm able to wrap my hand around it and pull the dead fuck into a sitting position after finally getting the lab coat's tail pulled up over his ass. After that, the job of getting the coat free of his arms and pulled away from his torso suddenly gets a lot easier.

There's a solid weight in one of the coat's pockets. I let go of the doc's tie, allowing the torso to flop back to the floor as I check out what's in that pocket. My hand dips into it and my fingers close around something slim and metallic. It's a shape I instantly recognize. If my soul had a shape, it would be this one. I'm smiling as I extract the flask from the pocket. The top is screwed on tight. I give it a little shake. The flask feels almost full. I screw off the cap and bring the opening to my nose for a sniff.

Smells like bourbon.

The good stuff. Really expensive.

I lower the flask, frowning as I stare at it. It's been a good while since I've tasted alcohol of any kind. Drinking booze used to be my favorite thing in the world. No, wait. Fucking Crazy Sue was my favorite thing in the world, back when I was still allowed to do the things normal humans do. I sigh and shiver at the memory of how good that was. She was crazy as fuck, but she brought me to heights of ecstasy no one else could ever match, and she did it countless times. The word "amazing" gets overused, but Crazy Sue really was amazing.

Booze, though.

Booze definitely ranks a close second.

Despite my recent encounter with her ghost, Crazy Sue is gone. She's dead. I'll never have what I used to have with her again. If I somehow get out of here and manage to survive for a while, maybe there'll be another woman to fuck someday. But she won't be Crazy Sue. I won't ever know that carnal level of amazing again.

But this bourbon.

It's right here. I can smell it. If I want, I can put it to my mouth and taste it. I can do it *right fucking now.* There's no good reason I shouldn't. The world is ending. Who the fuck cares if my long-dormant alcoholism kicks back into high gear the moment I have my first delicious taste of this divine nectar? And yet I hesitate. If I really want to survive beyond this day, getting drunk probably isn't the best idea.

I give the flask another shake.

I laugh softly.

Shit, motherfucker. I used to drink several times this amount every night. Okay, yeah, I'm a diminished fucking version of what I once was, but I can still handle this. I think. If I'm wrong, so what? Probably gonna die soon, anyway.

I bring the flask to my mouth and take that first taste. It's a sip. I groan in pleasure at the sweet, sweet fucking burn of it on my tongue. Just as I suspected, it's the good stuff. Not just from the top shelf, but from the secret back room at the liquor store where they keep the shit that goes for several hundred dollars a bottle. This dead doc was a rich motherfucker. I feel like I can clearly taste every precious penny of it as the first nip sits there on my tongue. Raising the flask, I silently salute the dead bourgeois bastard whose expensive taste in booze made this beautiful fucking moment possible. It's kind of too bad the guy is no longer among the living. I'd like to quiz him about the brand and maybe go on a liquor store raid once I've successfully made my way out of this place.

Then I bring the flask back to my mouth and take another taste of liquid gold. And another. Before I know it, I've downed half of its glorious fucking contents. I sit there for a while and allow the effect to slowly kick in as the liquor begins to circulate through my bloodstream. It doesn't take long to realize my tolerance level is nowhere near what it was in my glory days. I start feeling pretty drunk within about twenty minutes. At that point, I close the flask and set the rest of it aside for later.

Time to get back to the business of shedding the dead doc of his clothes. The rest of it goes much faster and isn't so much of a horrendous struggle. I feel strangely invigorated, as if the bourbon is a magical elixir that has restored a necessary balance within me. It's like I'm Drunk Popeye and booze is my fucking spinach. In the midst of this feeling, I resolve to never again have a sober minute should I actually manage to make good my escape.

Once I've managed to remove the dead man's pants from his body, I see they aren't quite in pristine condition. The man voided his bowels at the moment of death. Fortunately, most of the mess was absorbed by his underwear. The stain at the seat of his pants is nothing compared to my horrendous, shit-encrusted jumpsuit. Still, might as well take the time to clean the pants while I can. This part of the hospital appears to be a zombie-free zone. Failing to take full advantage of that would be colossally stupid on a level even beyond the many other acts of colossal stupidity I've been guilty of during my time on this stupid fucking planet. It means I can take as long as necessary to ensure I'm as prepared as possible before venturing back into more dangerous territory.

I search the exam room and find a plastic bottle of rubbing alcohol in a cabinet. Some clean white cloths turn up in a drawer. Using these, I manage to almost entirely scrub away the shit stain from the newly liberated pants. The pants I hang over the top of the exam table to dry. I inspect the rest of the dead man's clothes and judge them clean enough. I fold these items and set them aside.

And then the moment of truth is at hand. Well, not the whole truth. Like, on a universal, philosophical level. Instead, this is the latest in the endless succession of more mundane fucking truths we're all forced to face on a soul-deadening daily fucking basis until the day we die. It is time to remove the jumpsuit and see exactly how filthy and disgusting I really am beneath it.

So, I remove the thing. And it isn't easy. The part of it around my nether regions has to be carefully peeled away. Hairs come away from my body. A lot of hairs. Pubic hairs, many of them. I'm sorry, but there is no delicate or un-gross way of putting that. I feel sick. I struggle not to throw up, this despite the fact that my beleaguered fucking stomach must be absolutely devoid of anything of substance to expel at this point. That doesn't stop my guts from knotting. It doesn't keep the bile out of my throat. But this has to be done, so I grit my teeth and choke back the bile as I finish freeing myself of the horribly defiled garment. It so sickens me I can't be in the same room with it even another moment longer.

But where to put the disgusting goddamn thing?

After thinking about it a moment, I take the jumpsuit out of the exam room and glance up and down the hallway. Multiple other doors are standing open to either side of it. I go to the closest one. Another exam room, only there are no dead people in this one. I toss the soiled jumpsuit in there and rejoin the dead guys in the other room. I test the water tap at the sink. A stream of cold, clean water hits the bottom of the sink. This doesn't surprise me. The power was still on, after all. It makes sense the water is still there, too. I nonetheless heave a huge sigh of relief at the sight of it. I grab the rest of those clean white cloths and get to work scrubbing away the shit and urine from my groin, legs, and the crack of my ass. One by one, those clean cloths turn a sickening shade of deep, dark brown. I taste bile again multiple more times. But I force it down each time and stay focused on the disgusting but necessary task of cleaning myself. The cloths on hand are not nearly enough to finish the job. Big fucking surprise, right? I raid a couple of the other exam rooms for more. By the time I finally judge myself clean enough, more than forty-five minutes have passed. I know this thanks to the clock on the wall. Judging from the position of minute and hour hands, it's mid-afternoon. I have no idea what time of year it is. Depending on the season, I could have anywhere from two to four hours of daylight remaining.

This presents a dilemma.

I could try to head out now, or I could hole up in one of these rooms and wait for morning. On a cold, logical level, there's a lot to be said for waiting. This is a safe place. Or so it appears. I can make a full circuit of this section of the hospital to confirm it really is sealed off from the undead, but I think it's safe. If I stay here through the night, it's not likely anything can get in and hurt me. Then in the morning I could head out with a whole day of daylight ahead of me. This would almost undoubtedly be smarter than trying to navigate a post-apocalyptic fucking landscape at night.

The flipside to this is gut, animal instinct. That primal place inside where logic doesn't fucking exist. It's this part of me that recoils from the notion of voluntarily staying in this hellhole even one second longer than absolutely goddamn necessary. It isn't long before I understand that cold logic will hold no sway whatsoever over this powerful impulse. The idea of staying makes me want to crawl out of my fucking skin. I can't imagine cowering in here and trying to sleep through the night while knowing how close at hand freedom is. In that moment, it doesn't even matter how unlikely I am to find safe refuge before nightfall. More than anything else, I want to be gone from this place forever.

So, fuck it.

I'm heading out.

PART VII
COMPLICATIONS

I PUT ON THE DEAD man's clothes and find the fit even worse than expected. I'm like a stick-man with a tent draped over his body. Or a small child trying on his father's clothes. Still, it's a monumental improvement over the alternative of continuing to marinate in my own waste. I feel almost human again. And at least I've got the belt to keep the pants from sliding down my narrow, bony hips. I'll worry about finding better-fitting clothes after I'm out of here, assuming my attempt at escape is successful.

Which it better fucking well be, because I'm out of other options.

Before I go, I take the flask and the dead doc's gun with me. Both go in the billowing pockets of the liberated jeans. My initial instinct is to tuck the gun in the waistband at the small of my back. You know, like people are always doing in movies, but when the gun slides into the seat of the pants I've commandeered, I rethink the idea. Tightening the belt even further to prevent this would require creating new notches in the leather and I have no interest in taking the time to do this. Another couple items are already in those pockets, the dead man's wallet and the keys to his car. The wallet contains a few hundred dollars in cash. That would have been a lot of money to me in the good old days, almost like a fucking fortune. Now, though? It's probably worthless. It's the end of the world out there, which means there's almost certainly nothing like a functioning economy anymore. Still, it can't hurt to take the money with me. Just in case. Same goes for the car keys. I'll need transportation if I want to put some serious distance between myself and this shithole. The electronic fob is embossed with a BMW logo. Finding the doc's car won't be easy, but at least that helps narrow things down.

When I'm sure I'm as prepared as I can be, I head back the way I came a little while ago. I return to the empty breakroom and crack open the door to the stairwell. As best I can tell, it's still empty, at least on this level. Time to go. I let out a breath and slip out into the stairwell. As I start to ease the door shut, my hand freezes around the doorknob. The hesitation is another thing that occurs at the primal level. There's no immediately obvious reason for it. My brow furrows as wheels start to spin in my head. Then my eyes widen as the conscious part of my brain catches up to the subconscious impulse that led to this moment.

I think about the idea taking shape in my head. It makes sense. I never did a full circuit of the section of the hospital I was on the verge of permanently vacating. So, the thing I'm envisioning is definitely possible. Hell, maybe even likely. There's a keypad on the wall next to the door. The potted plant holding the door open had been kicked aside. By me, obviously. If I'd allowed the door to close, I never would have been able to get back in there. Which would be a shame, if what I'm thinking is right. Part of me is freaking out inside at this hesitation. It's the paranoid part focused on the dwindling daylight. I shouldn't be wasting time exploring every random goddamn notion that occurs to me. And there's some pretty serious validity to this side of it, without a fucking doubt. Still, now that the idea is in my head, I can't let it go without visual confirmation one way or the other.

Goddammit.

I pull the door open again and slip back inside, pulling the door all the way shut again. A zombie getting into this section seems unlikely at this point, and the door would shut of its own accord within a few seconds, anyway, but it doesn't hurt anything to take the precaution. As soon as I'm sure the door can't be opened again from the outside, I turn away from it and hurry back through the breakroom and down the hallway beyond at the fastest rate I can manage, which, let me fucking tell you, isn't nearly as fast as I'd like. Beyond the far end of the corridor is a slightly larger area. When I get there, I sigh in relief as I immediately see what I was expecting to find.

Two sets of elevator doors.

A panel of up and down buttons on the wall between them.

I press the fucking down button.

Obviously.

This is what came to me in the last second out there in the stairwell. In a section of the facility frequented by high-level staff, there would have to be a goddamn elevator. A bunch of pampered doctors aren't gonna stand for a situation in which they're constantly having to go up and down a bunch of goddamn stairs. In the normal course of things, I'd have a sneering, self-righteous attitude about that shit, but right about now I'm thankful as hell for the entrenched, institutional laziness that made this moment possible. You see, a faint part of me knows the impression of reinvigoration is nothing but booze-induced delusion. The stark reality is I'm still a debilitated shell of my former fucking self. Maybe that stairwell was empty all the way to the ground floor, but I can't know that, not without descending the stairs to find out. It's possible there are zombies on the lower landings, and the prospect of fighting my way through them in my condition isn't all that goddamn enticing, to say the fucking least.

So, given the option, I'll take the elevator instead. I mean, yeah, I'll have to tangle with zombies again soon enough, but at least this will increase my chances of safely getting out of the building first. This is what I'm thinking as an arrival chime sounds and a light above the door on the left flashes a bright yellow. I'm already stepping toward the elevator as the door begins to slide open.

But then I stop in my tracks.

"Oh, shit," I say, reaching into my pocket for the gun.

The elevator is full of dead fuckers. My heart is hammering like a motherfucker as the sight of the gun snags on the inner lining of the pocket. There's a sharp pain at the center of my chest that might be worrisome under other circumstances. That is, circumstances in which I am not in imminent danger of being eaten alive by a pack of starving, flesh-hungry ghouls. The elevator is packed with them. It's wall-to-wall reanimated dead. My estimate is ten or more based on a quick visual scan. The local fire marshal would not be happy with this level of overcrowding. I'm not too crazy about it, either.

Ironically, the sheer number of them is part of what saves me. They're all wedged in there too tightly to maneuver around effectively. Most of them aren't even aware of me at first. A lot of them are tangled up with each other or facing the wall instead of looking out at my wide-eyed, terrified mug. And even by dead fucker standards, this gaggle of dead things is pretty fucking listless. An awful stench wafts out of the elevator. They've been in there a while, maybe since the start of this outbreak. One set of milky dead eyes at last turns in my direction and appears to semi-focus on me. A shaky hand reaches in my direction, grasping at the air. I keep desperately tugging at the gun, but the sight remains snagged on the fabric. Fortunately, it's just that one dead thing that seems aware of me as I continue fighting with the gun. He's trying to writhe free of the tangle of undead bodies, but it's proving difficult work. By then I'm thinking the time factor will wind up being my salvation here. Elevator doors don't stay open long, unless someone in there is keeping their finger on the "door open" button, and that doesn't seem likely. A few more seconds should be all it takes.

And, of course, as soon I have this thought, that's when the struggling zombie abruptly slips free of the rest of the tangled horde and comes staggering toward the open door. It's almost out of the elevator. I panic and take a reflexive step backward, still tugging at the gun, which at last comes loose with a sound of ripping fabric. The elevator doors at last begin to close. The doors briefly pin the zombie between them, then retract as the sensors detect its presence. But the zombie still isn't all the way out of the fucking elevator. It stands there on the threshold, its head wobbling about on its shoulder, body swaying back and forth. This goes on for several more seconds, and I stand there, hoping the goddamn thing will tumble backward, rejoining its undead kin. Instead, the elevator doors begin to come together again. The zombie is pinned a second time, but this time when the doors retract, the creature tumbles forward, most of its body landing on the floor outside the elevator.

But its feet are still in there.

And now some of the other zombies are stirring, belatedly becoming aware of my presence. More sets of dead, milky eyes are turning in my direction.

"Fuck this shit," is what I say at this point.

Because, really, fuck the holy hell out of this shit.

Right?

I rush forward and snag a handful of the zombie's shirt collar. I grunt and tremble in exertion, sweat forming on my brow as I pull the goddamn thing clear of the elevator. The zombie tries clutching at me with a shaking hand. Fortunately, it seems as weak as me, having been deprived of warm human flesh for who knows how the fuck long. Brushing the hand aside, I step back, aim the gun at the crown of its skull, and squeeze the trigger. The volume of the gun's report makes me flinch and the recoil makes me stagger backward several steps. It's a miracle that I manage to hold on to it at all. There's now a mess of zombie brains and blood on the floor, but the creature is no longer moving. That's one threat neutralized.

Unfortunately, there are more ready to take its place.

Another zombie has slipped loose of the mass of flesh and is on the brink of emerging from the elevator. At least one more looks like it's right on the verge of doing the same.

"Fuck this shit," I say again.

Again, I rush forward, and this time I shove the lead zombie in the chest, causing it to flail uselessly and topple back into the elevator. Before it can get righted and come at me again, I aim the gun at its head, this time making sure to take hold of the gun's grip in both hands before squeezing the trigger. The second report of the gun also makes me flinch, but this time I'm prepared for the recoil and only get knocked back a few inches as a spray of blood and dumb zombie brains rains down on all the other dumb fucking zombies in there. The elevator doors begin to slide shut again. This time there's nothing to block them and make them bounce open again. And just as they finally close, I hear that nauseatingly cheery chime again.

The other elevator is opening now.

I groan.

I say, "Goddammit."

This one will be empty, I tell myself. *You're finally going to catch a break. This is your reward for the struggle you've just endured.*

You'll no doubt be unsurprised to learn what a gargantuan load of fucking bullshit that inner pronouncement was.

I shuffle over to the right a few steps to stand before it as the doors come open. My gun is upraised. It occurs to me I have no idea how many bullets still remain in the magazine. I didn't bother to pop it out and count them before setting out on an escape attempt that thus far could generously be described as not going quite as smoothly as it could be.

The doors are open.

There are more zombies in there.

Of fucking course.

One comes lurching out right away. It's considerably more lively than the two I've shot. As it comes at me with surprising speed, it makes a sound like a growl and bares its teeth. It's possible I whimpered at that point. Not even gonna lie. I was scared and maybe a moment away from death. I exert pressure on the trigger, grimacing as I really bear down on it. It feels like it's taking forever to squeeze off that shot. The fucking zombie is almost upon me. It's three feet away.

Two.

One.

Then, *Boom.*

More blood. More brains.

The zombie corpse nonetheless takes its time falling over. I give it an assist with a hard shove. It's out of the way in time for me to shoot the next undead fucker following in the first one's wake. This second one falls backward, landing half in and half out of the elevator. The doors try to slide shut, but bounce back again. More zombies are trying to come out of the elevator. By the time I can haul the one I've just killed out of the way, they'll be out here and coming after me.

Fuck it.

I'm not gonna be able to contain this.

I turn away from the elevator and start running back down the hallway to the breakroom. Not quite halfway down the corridor, I feel my right foot slide forward a faster than the left foot. It's the fault of the dead man's expensive boat shoes. They are decidedly not meant for running at high speed, especially not on a slightly slick surface like the floor of this hallway. I'm off balance and right away I'm flailing about like a fucking spaz in an attempt to stabilize myself before I take a spill. The attempt is spectacularly unsuccessful. The spill happens. I land hard on my ass. The gun flies out of my hand and goes spinning away on the polished white floor tiles. That landing hurts. I scream in pain. You would, too, if you had as little backside cushioning as I do now. On the floor and unable to see them from my current vantage point, I hear the groaning and lurching of the zombies. They're close. Too fucking close. Staying where I am and allowing the pain time to recede isn't an option. I have to push through it, goddammit.

Screaming again—this time through gritted teeth—I roll over, brace my hands on the tiles beneath me, and begin to push myself up off the floor. By the time I manage to get all the way upright, the nearest zombie is maybe six feet away. Several more are right behind him. Because I'm still a touch woozy from the fall, I brace a hand against the wall to my right to keep from immediately falling over again as I spin away from them. The gun is about a dozen feet ahead of me. When I get close to it, I bend to scoop it up. It's in my fingers for a fraction of a second, but it tumbles away again before I can secure my grip on it.

I scream an expletive.

What a dumb fucking word.

"Expletive."

Jesus.

I scream, *"Fuck!"*

This time the gun has spun through an open exam room door. It's just inside the doorway. Thankfully. Otherwise I might have written the goddamn thing off as lost. I get to the door and bend to scoop it up again, this time taking that extra second or two necessary to get a good hold on the fucker. This time I don't drop it, but it's almost at the cost of my life.

The nearest zombie has reached me. I feel ragged fingernails grasping at my shirt sleeve. Spinning toward the thing, I drill an elbow into the center of its face, pulping its nose. A burst of blood stains my shirt. This pisses me off. I've just obtained the goddamn thing and already the fucking zombie apocalypse is making a mess of it.

C'est la fucking vie.

I press the gun against the zombie's forehead and squeeze the trigger. It drops to the floor, but there are more right behind it. Too many. That second elevator was as full as the first, but it appears the zombies packed into it are livelier in general than those others were. And faster. I mean, they're still slow shamblers, make no mistake, but there's no denying they've got a bit more spring in their step. Even in the midst of this struggle to live, I can't help but spend a moment wondering what the story was behind the elevator zombies. Did they become zombies before they went into the elevators or after? It could be they were dead fuckers already and were herded into the elevators by a contingent of the living in a doomed effort to contain what was happening. I guess I could see that, but my money's on an alternate scenario. I base this on the way so many of those poor bastards were wedged into those things. They were still alive, all of them, and they were desperate for a place to hide, but something went wrong. Maybe they were in there a while, listening to the sounds of the dawning apocalypse raging outside those closed doors. Maybe long enough that they slept. And while they slept, one among them died. That's all it would have taken. Just one to die and turn into a dead fuck. And you can imagine easily enough the gory chain reaction that would have followed.

Sounds right to me, but there's no way to fucking know, is there? It's not like I can quiz any of these undead pieces of shit about it. And, anyway, I feel kind of sorry for them, but their story isn't my story, except for this slice of it that intersects with mine.

I adjust my aim and squeeze the trigger again, killing the next closest zombie.

There's enough space between me and the rest of them now that I feel safe turning away from them and resuming my flight back down the hallway. This time I jog instead of run, hoping to avoid a repeat of my previous tumble, because another one might be the end of me. But that doesn't happen. I get to the breakroom and reach the door to the stairwell. It's only been a few minutes since the last time I opened this door, but it feels kind of like a fucking lifetime. I've wasted a lot of precious time. My regret over the impulse to check out the elevators runs deep. If I hadn't done that, I might have been out of here already. It was a mistake. On the other hand, there's no way I could have known that ahead of time. There had been logic behind the idea. It'd seemed sensible in that moment. Only in retrospect did it seem otherwise.

However, the experience *did* teach me a valuable lesson, one I should have learned a long time ago.

Never take anything for granted.

This time I ease the door open a bit more carefully than the last time. Not too slowly, because those undead cocksuckers are still coming after me, but slowly enough to hopefully prepare myself for any threat that might be lurking out there in the stairwell. It was empty the last time I checked, as you might fucking remember, if you had a fucking brain in your head, but that doesn't mean that'll still be the case. It's possible some zombies from a lower level have ascended to check out the commotion.

I peek through the slim crack between the door and the edge of the doorframe.

Still empty.

Or so it seems.

I pull the door the rest of the way open and there you are again, lurking off to the side, giggling in the corner with a can of beer in your hand.

The fucking devil.

Goddammit.

PART VIII
FEAR AND LOATHING AT
THE END OF THE WORLD

"YOU AGAIN."

I say it deadpan, my features twisted in an expression of tired disbelief.

The devil grins and takes a swig from his beer as he pushes away from the wall. "Hey. How's it hanging, *mi compadre?*"

"Fuck you."

The door clicks shut behind me. I'm finally safe from the pack of zombies I inadvertently freed from that second elevator. It's clear, though, that true safety is still out of reach.

Maybe for good.

And, listen, before we go any further, for the sake of relative clarity, I'll refrain from addressing you directly for the remainder of this account. You'll go back to being just another character in my story.

For now.

You fucking asshole.

Okay, *now* I'll refrain from addressing you directly.

Sorry, couldn't help myself.

Anyway, it's I-don't-know-how-many-years-later since I last saw this grinning cockface, but he's still wearing the same obnoxiously loud outfit. Red and white Hawaiian shirt hanging open over a hairy potbelly. Cargo shorts and flip-flops. Wide-brimmed white Panama hat tipped low over his forehead. His skin is tinged a dusty shade of crimson most would mistake for a deep tan from a distance. Beneath the Panama hat, as I've seen before, are a couple of nubby little horns. The devil looks like a tourist from the Midwest trying to fit in while on vacation in fucking Key West.

If I were a devoted Satanist, I would be one disappointed motherfucker.

Obnoxious appearance aside, this is definitely the devil. Beelzebub. Ol' Scratch. His Satanic fucking majesty. And he's every bit as evil and diabolical as his reputation would have you believe. Hell, this ugly piece of shit is the reason I've lost a chunk of my life to the looney bin.

I raise the gun and point it at his face.

The devil keeps on grinning and shakes his head. "Come now. Do you really think that'll hurt me?"

Recalling the time I tried to punch the devil in the fucking face—it felt like slamming my fist against concrete—I lower the gun and let out a weary breath.

"What are you doing here?"

The devil takes another swig of beer. It's Schlitz, like last time. I can't remember the last time I even saw motherfucking Schlitz in a store. I'm not even sure they still make that shit. But, hey, this is the devil. He's got his ways of procuring whatever he wants, I'm sure.

"I'm here to help you."

I laugh.

The devil finishes his beer and crushes the empty can in his hand. A flip of his hand sends the can rattling down the stairwell. He snaps his fingers and a fresh can appears in the same hand. Magic. Like I said, motherfucker has his ways. He pops the tab on the can and there's a familiar hiss I haven't heard in way too long. It elicits an unexpected pang of melancholy. I've still got the rest of that expensive bourbon in the pilfered flask, but there's really nothing like an ice-cold beer.

"Oh, I'm sorry. Would *you* like a beer?"

I frown.

The obvious answer is *yes*, but . . .

"Is that even real beer? How can it be, when you make it appear out of thin air like that? It's an illusion. An infernal Jedi mind trick. Got to be."

The devil chuckles. "Oh, it's real. You've got my word on that. I'd try telling you how I do it, but it'd be like trying to explain quantum physics to a puppy. And not even like a purebred puppy. More like a mongrel pound puppy. A *retarded* mongrel pound puppy."

"Did you come here just to insult me? Really?"

The devil's grin disappears. This is a strange thing to see. Until now, that grin had seemed permanently affixed to his ugly fucking face. His expression turns serious. As anyone else out there could probably imagine, this development is more than slightly disturbing. A bizarrely jovial and poorly attired epitome of pure fucking evil I can almost kind of handle. The lighthearted veneer allows for a buffering distance from the truth of the thing, but when the veneer drops, shit starts to feel a little too real.

It feels *demonic*.

I can almost smell the brimstone seeping into the air.

"I'm not here to insult you, buddy. Well, not *just* for that. I like you, believe it or not. We're buds. Bros. We've partied together, shared some good times. We've both rutted in the same sloppy mess of intestines. No, the actual reason I'm here has to do with Crazy Sue. And you."

I feel a bit queasy at the reference to our joint defilement of my dead lover's body. Choking down bile, I manage to continue. "That's not quite how I'd describe what happened, but let's set that aside for now. What about Crazy Sue?"

The devil gulps beer. He belches. "I sensed a disturbance in the Force." There's a twitch of a grin at the corners of his mouth, but it fades quickly. "Or the equivalent thereof in Hell. See, I can make with the *Star Wars* references, too. I told you, we're simpatico. Anyway, I can tell when someone's trying to tap into infernal power. And I'm not talking about some teenaged wannabe me worshipper invoking my name in some half-assed spell or summoning. I mean the real deal, an attempt to hijack and redirect the underlying power of Hell itself. It doesn't happen very often for the simple reason that doing it is next to impossible. Since the dawn of time, it's only happened one other time. That's how fucking rare it is. So, naturally, I took a keen interest in tracking down the responsible party. Didn't take long. I *am* the devil, after all. And Hell is my playground. You can't go mucking around in there without me finding out about it. And do you want to know who my investigation revealed as the perpetrator?"

It isn't hard to figure out where this is going. "Crazy Sue?"

The devil smiles and nods. "Hey, good for you. You are absolutely, one-hundred percent correct. Maybe you're not so dumb, after all."

I ignore the insult and say, "But how could Crazy Sue do a thing like that? She's dead."

The devil chuckles. "Don't be so provincial. Dead on the physical plane doesn't mean gone forever or non-existent. Sue's noncorporeal essence is still out there. At the time of death, souls are assigned either to purgatory or heaven or hell. A few are left in limbo and become what you dumb mortals think of as ghosts."

"And that's what Sue is? A ghost?"

"That's right, buddy. Damn, you're getting quicker on the uptake all the time. You're still not quite Mensa material, but you could be on the verge of graduating from the short bus."

Again, I ignore the insult. Not because I'm above such crassness. Trading insults and being a rude dick in general is right in my fucking wheelhouse. I'm good at it. But I don't bother this time because I'm too stunned by this final confirmation that I hadn't been hallucinating after emerging from the drug haze in the cell. Sue really had been in there with me. Or, rather, her ghost had been in there with me.

I let out a breath and shake my head. "Holy shit."

The devil gulps beer and wipes foam from his mouth. "Indeed. And it seems the incorporeal bitch still has a soft spot for you, which, call me old-fashioned, seems kind of odd considering it was you who cut her belly open and started that whole thing of rolling around in her offal and getting turned on by it."

I glare at him. "Fuck you. That only happened because you fucked with my head somehow. I wouldn't have done something that fucking perverted otherwise."

The devil grins and winks at me. "Are you sure about that?"

My glare intensifies. "I'm pretty fucking sure, asshole. So, you're here to track down Sue? Well, don't expect me to help with that, because I won't. I don't even care how much you torture or threaten me. It is not fucking happening. You hear me?"

A smirk tugs at a corner of the infernal douchebag's mouth. "Damn, I don't know, you should be careful with statements like that. You keep forgetting that I am Evil Incarnate. I am ancient. I am eternal. My wrath is terrible beyond your comprehension. And so on and so forth. Anyway, I'm not here to torture or threaten you. Like I said, we're pals. I mean that most sincerely. And, anyway, I don't need to find Sue. I only needed to identify the source of the hack, which I did. And now her access to my power has been permanently blocked. No, I'm not worried about her at all. She's free to flit about on this miserable fucking plane without fear of reprisal from me forever, as far as I'm concerned."

Confusion displaces some of my anger. "Okay. Let's say I believe that. Then why in fuck are you here?"

The devil finishes off his second beer and again crushes the empty in his hand. This one also goes rattling down the stairwell. He snaps his fingers and yet another replacement appears out of fucking nowhere. He sighs as he pops the tab on the new can. There's an unmistakable tinge of sadness in the sound. "I told you right at the start, I'm here to help you. You really need to work on your listening skills."

"Why would you want to help me?"

The devil groans loudly and rolls his head about on his shoulders in apparent deep exasperation. "Dude, I've *told* you this, too. A bunch of fucking times. I meant what I said. We're friends. I feel like we bonded in a real and very deep way when we made that glorious fucking mess of Crazy Sue. And I know you felt the same at the time. You even came out and said it, but you were so wasted off your ass that you don't remember."

I shake my head. "This is such unmitigated bullshit."

"It isn't."

"It is."

"Is not."

"Is."

"Is not times infinity. Now shut the fuck up. Time to get you out of here."

He abruptly seizes me by an arm and mutters words in a language I don't understand. A nauseatingly thick-headed feeling suffuses every bit of my being for an awful-beyond-comprehension fraction of a second. Then there's a brief blank period. It's like I'm in a dreamless void. No idea how long it lasts. Maybe an instant. Maybe an eternity. Who the fuck knows and what difference does it make at this point?

The world and existence itself have simply *gone away*.

Then it's back.

And with it, a momentarily jarring sense of displacement, because now we're outside on the grounds of the facility. This is at the rear of the building, in the employee parking lot I glimpsed earlier when looking out that stairwell window. Only now there's a car down here I didn't see before. It's a vintage red Mustang from the late 60s. A convertible with a white top, which is down now. In the back are two gorgeous women clad only in tiny bikinis. One's a blonde, the other a redhead. The blonde has enormous floppy tits. They jiggle every time she laughs, which is a lot. She and her companion are having a whispered conversation punctuated by constant giggles. Each woman is drinking some manner of alcoholic concoction from a cocktail glass.

Zombies are milling about in the lot, but none of them are within several feet of the Mustang. The dead fuckers don't even attempt to approach the vehicle. Which is weird. It's as if there's some kind of invisible protective bubble around it. And, hell, there probably is.

Some of the zombies turn our way when we appear.

They begin to stagger toward us.

The devil waves his hand and they fall over.

I've got to admit, it's pretty impressive.

The devil takes a swig of beer and glances at me. "What do you say? Want to hit the road with me and the girls?"

I frown. "Where would we go?"

The devil laughs and waves an arm around. "Anywhere. Everywhere. It's the apocalypse out there, buddy. There's a whole world of fun, fucked-up shit to see. It'll be an adventure. A road trip for the ages. I've been meaning to get away from it all for a while. Running things in Hell has gotten kind of stale after so many millennia. I'd like to spend a few years running wild here on earth. And, hey, look at those girls. Smoking hot, aren't they? How long has it been since you got laid?"

I think about it. "Um . . . I don't know. I don't even know how long I was in this place."

The devil shrugs. "Me either. Hey, I would have come for you sooner, but I got preoccupied and distracted by all kinds of shit. You know how it is. Anyway, those babes are yours for the taking any time you feel like it. And there's more where they came from.

An endless supply. Come on, man. That's gotta sound pretty fucking awesome after what you've been through. Right?"

I can't deny it.

I don't fully believe everything else he's told me, but he's right about that. It *does* sound pretty fucking awesome. I'm sure there's some sinister underlining behind his motives for inviting me to come along on this trip, but I decide I don't care. The world is over. Everyone and everything I've ever cared about is gone. I decide to accept the devil's invitation. What else would I do?

I shrug. "Whatever, man. Fuck it. Let's go."

The devil laughs heartily and claps a hand on my shoulder. "My man! You are not going to regret this decision. I promise you. Good times await, buddy."

I nod. "If you say so."

"I *do* say so. And, hey, don't forget this other perk."

He tosses back the rest of his beer and throws the empty over his shoulder. Then he snaps his fingers and a new can appears in his hand. He passes it to me unopened. I accept it with only a slight degree of trepidation. Now that I've resigned myself to whatever eventual grim fate this creature has in mind for me, the idea of drinking magical beer no longer troubles me much. I pop the tab on the can and shiver in pleasure at the familiar sweet sound of air escaping.

There's nothing better than that sound.

I put the can to my mouth, tilt my head back, and drink deeply from it. By the time I take the can away from my mouth, more than half of its contents are gone.

And I'm smiling.

Hello, oblivion. My old friend.

The devil claps me on the shoulder again. "Good man. That's what I like about you. You don't drink like a pussy. And now . . . our chariot awaits!"

We get in the car.

The devil settles in behind the wheel and I climb into the back with the girls. They're all over me. Bikini tops disappear. I lose myself in their flesh. I'd describe it as heavenly, only that doesn't seem appropriate given the company I'm keeping now.

I'm in ecstasy as we drive off into the night.

That's weird.

It was still full daylight only a second ago, but now night has fallen. I'd worry about it, but the blonde is right on top of me by then and in that moment nothing else matters.

Up front, the devil is laughing.

BIO

Bryan Smith is the author of numerous novels and novellas, including *68 Kill*, *Slowly We Rot*, *Depraved*, *The Killing Kind*, *Last Day*, *Dead Stripper Storage*, *Dirty Rotten Hippies and Other Stories*, and *Kill For Satan!*, which won a Splatterpunk Award for best horror novella of 2018. Bestselling horror author Brian Keene described *Slowly We Rot* as, "The best zombie novel I've ever read." A film version of *68 Kill*, directed by Trent Haaga and starring Matthew Gray Gubler from *Criminal Minds*, was released in 2017. Bryan lives in Tennessee with his wife Jennifer and their many pets.

Follow him on Twitter at @Bryan_D_Smith and on Facebook at www.facebook.com/bryansmith/

Other Grindhouse Press Titles

#666__*Satanic Summer* by Andersen Prunty
#058__*True Crime* by Samantha Kolesnik
#057__*The Cycle* by John Wayne Comunale
#056__*A Voice So Soft* by Patrick Lacey
#055__*Merciless* by Bryan Smith
#054__*The Long Shadows of October* by Kristopher Triana
#053__*House of Blood* by Bryan Smith
#052__*The Freakshow* by Bryan Smith
#051__*Dirty Rotten Hippies and Other Stories* by Bryan Smith
#050__*Rites of Extinction* by Matt Serafini
#049__*Saint Sadist* by Lucas Mangum
#048__*Neon Dies at Dawn* by Andersen Prunty
#047__*Halloween Fiend* by C.V. Hunt
#046__*Limbs: A Love Story* by Tim Meyer
#045__*As Seen On T.V.* by John Wayne Comunale
#044__*Where Stars Won't Shine* by Patrick Lacey
#043__*Kinfolk* by Matt Kurtz
#042__*Kill For Satan!* by Bryan Smith
#041__*Dead Stripper Storage* by Bryan Smith
#040__*Triple Axe* by Scott Cole
#039__*Scummer* by John Wayne Comunale
#038__*Cockblock* by C.V. Hunt
#037__*Irrationalia* by Andersen Prunty
#036__*Full Brutal* by Kristopher Triana
#035__*Office Mutant* by Pete Risley
#034__*Death Pacts and Left-Hand Paths* by John Wayne Comunale
#033__*Home Is Where the Horror Is* by C.V. Hunt
#032__*This Town Needs A Monster* by Andersen Prunty
#031__*The Fetishists* by A.S. Coomer
#030__*Ritualistic Human Sacrifice* by C.V. Hunt
#029__*The Atrocity Vendor* by Nick Cato

#028__*Burn Down the House and Everyone In It* by Zachary T. Owen

#027__*Misery and Death and Everything Depressing* by C.V. Hunt

#026__*Naked Friends* by Justin Grimbol

#025__*Ghost Chant* by Gina Ranalli

#024__*Hearers of the Constant Hum* by William Pauley III

#023__*Hell's Waiting Room* by C.V. Hunt

#022__*Creep House: Horror Stories* by Andersen Prunty

#021__*Other People's Shit* by C.V. Hunt

#020__*The Party Lords* by Justin Grimbol

#019__*Sociopaths In Love* by Andersen Prunty

#018__*The Last Porno Theater* by Nick Cato

#017__*Zombieville* by C.V. Hunt

#016__*Samurai Vs. Robo-Dick* by Steve Lowe

#015__*The Warm Glow of Happy Homes* by Andersen Prunty

#014__*How To Kill Yourself* by C.V. Hunt

#013__*Bury the Children in the Yard: Horror Stories* by Andersen Prunty

#012__*Return to Devil Town (Vampires in Devil Town Book Three)* by Wayne Hixon

#011__*Pray You Die Alone: Horror Stories* by Andersen Prunty

#010__*King of the Perverts* by Steve Lowe

#009__*Sunruined: Horror Stories* by Andersen Prunty

#008__*Bright Black Moon (Vampires in Devil Town Book Two)* by Wayne Hixon

#007__*Hi I'm a Social Disease: Horror Stories* by Andersen Prunty

#006__*A Life On Fire* by Chris Bowsman

#005__*The Sorrow King* by Andersen Prunty

#004__*The Brothers Crunk* by William Pauley III

#003__*The Horribles* by Nathaniel Lambert

#002__*Vampires in Devil Town* by Wayne Hixon

#001__*House of Fallen Trees* by Gina Ranalli

#000__*Morning is Dead* by Andersen Prunty